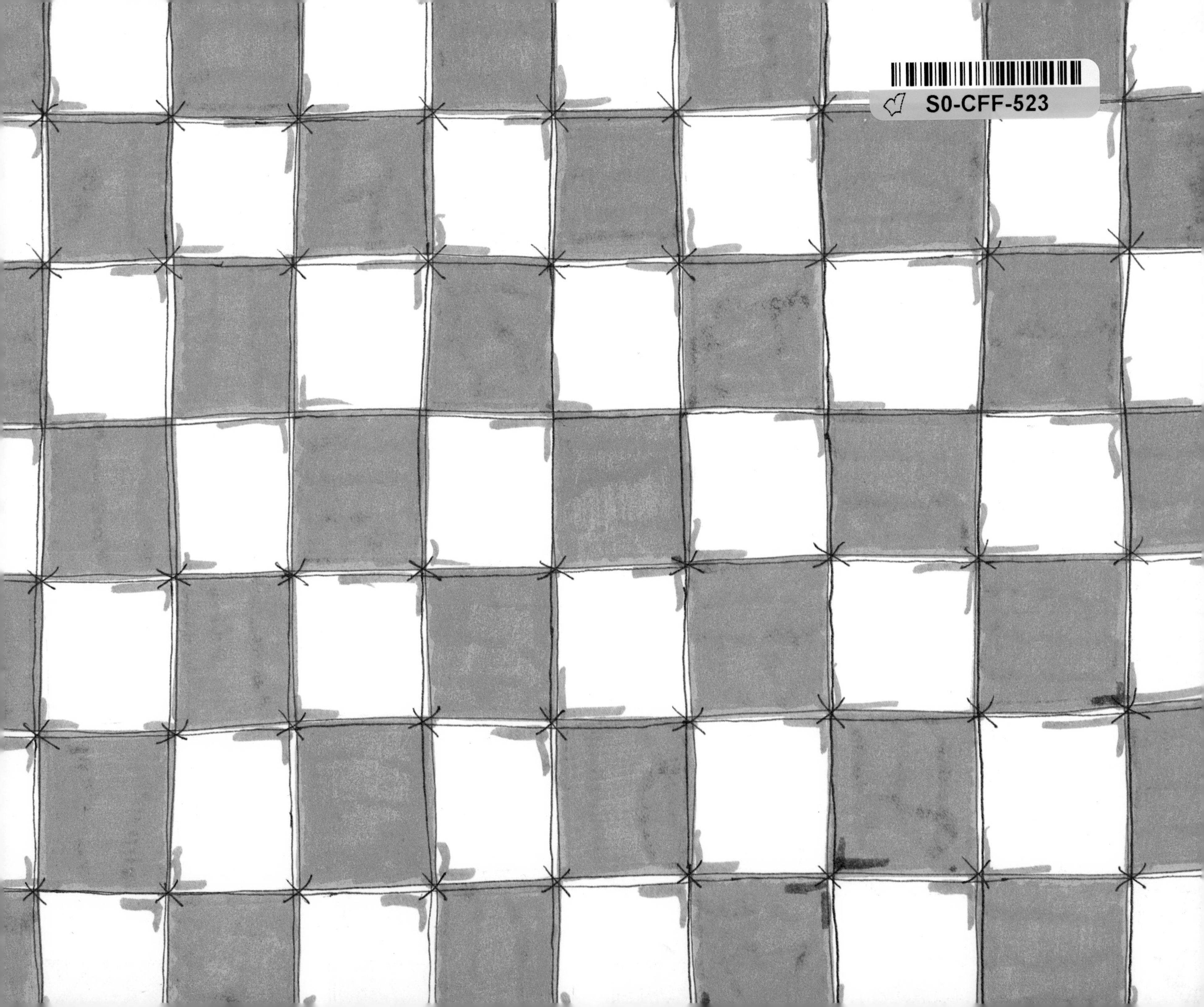

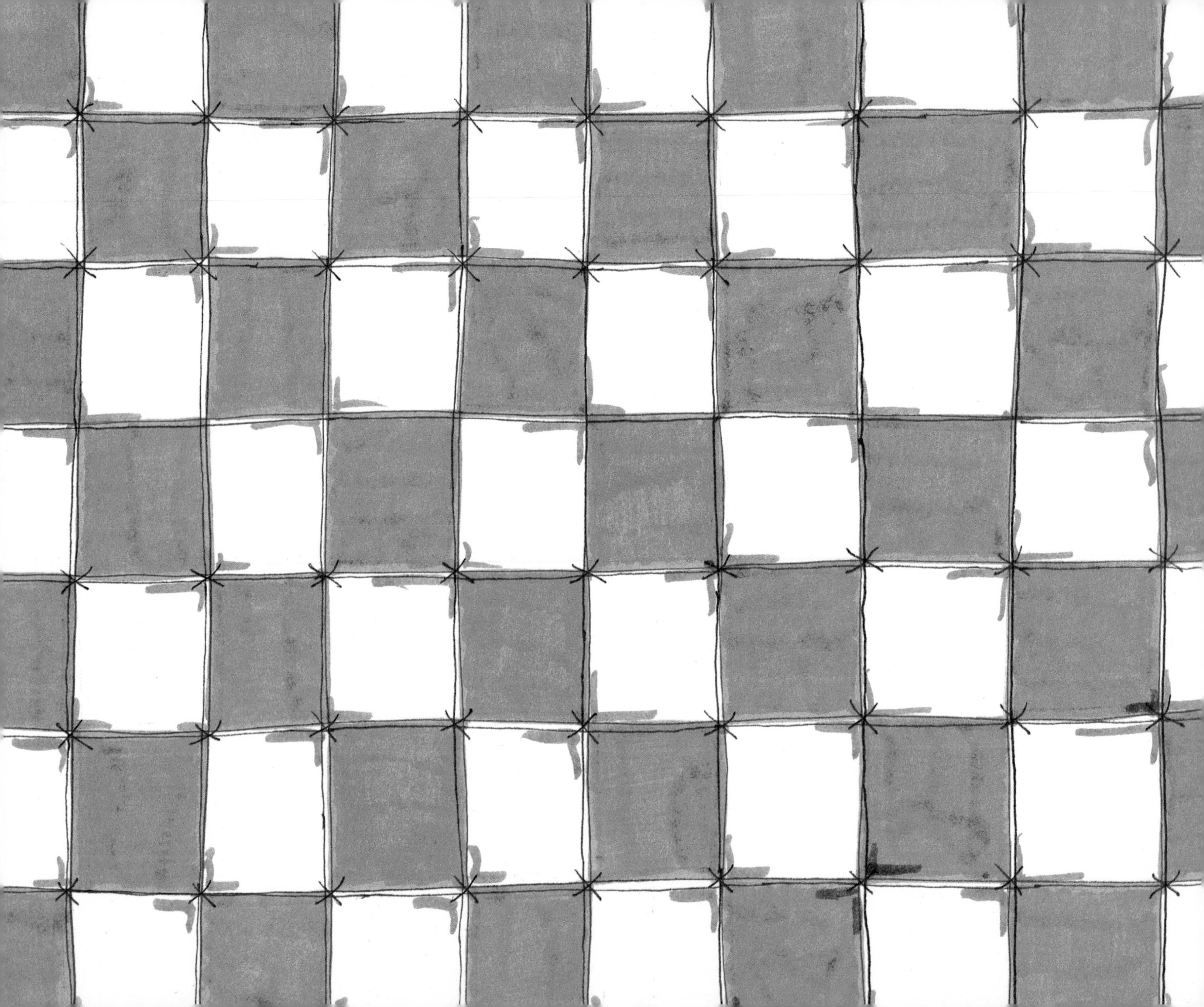

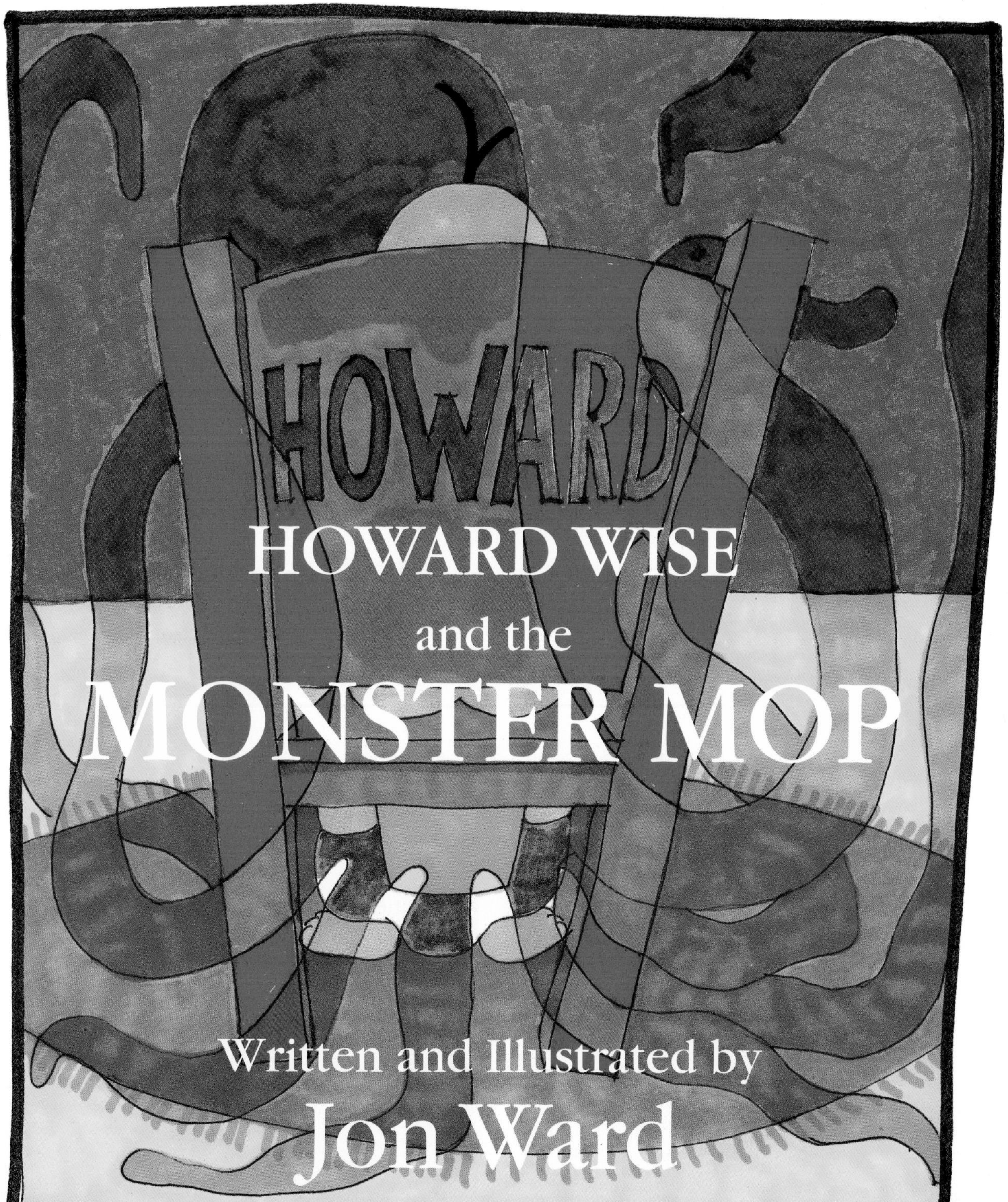
HOWARD

HOWARD WISE and the MONSTER MOP

Written and Illustrated by

Jon Ward

To All of the Great Women who have Encouraged and Prodded me along the Way, starting with my Mother.

Also by Jon Ward
The Clash of the Cowasorouses

Scanned and Typeset at Georgia Litho, Atlanta, Ga.. Thanks, Guys.

First Edition

ISBN-0-9658128-0-4
Library of Congress Cataloging-in-Publication Data 97-093588

Ward, Jon.
  Howard Wise and the Monster Mop.

Summary: A sneaky monster makes a huge mess, and, in attempting to shift the blame to Howard, is taught a valuable lesson.
  1. Monsters-Fiction   2. Bathroom Stories-Fiction
  3. Humorous Stories-Fiction   I. Title.

Printed in Hong Kong

Long Wind Publishing
2208 River Branch Drive, Ft. Pierce, Florida, 34981
561-595-0268 fax 561-595-6246

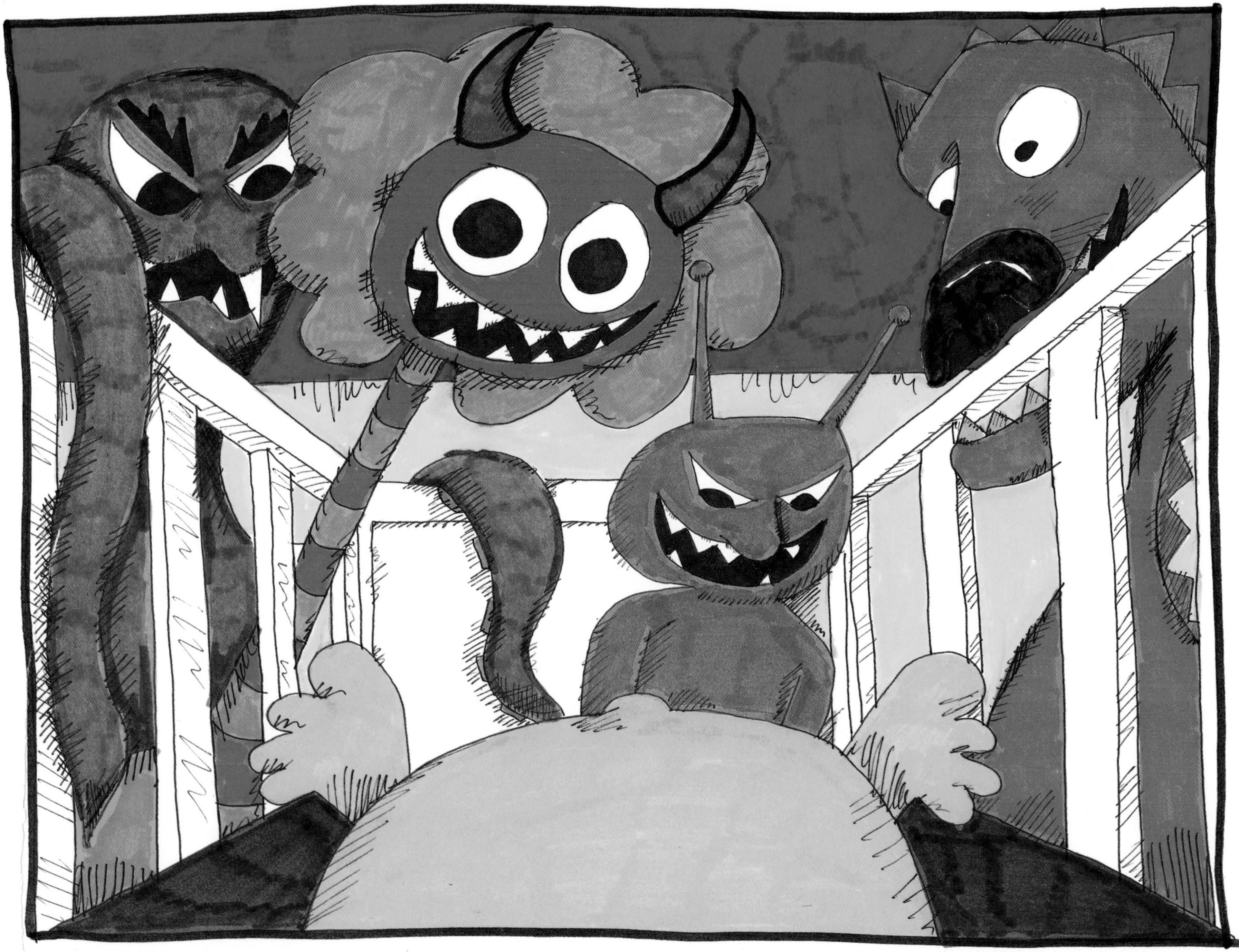

Howard Wise was a kid who had this really creepy feeling that there might be lots of monsters in the world.

It was because everything was so very BIG. This stuff couldn't have bee
made for kids. It had to be made for something big, like MONSTERS.
Really big ones. Yeah.

There MUST be monsters.

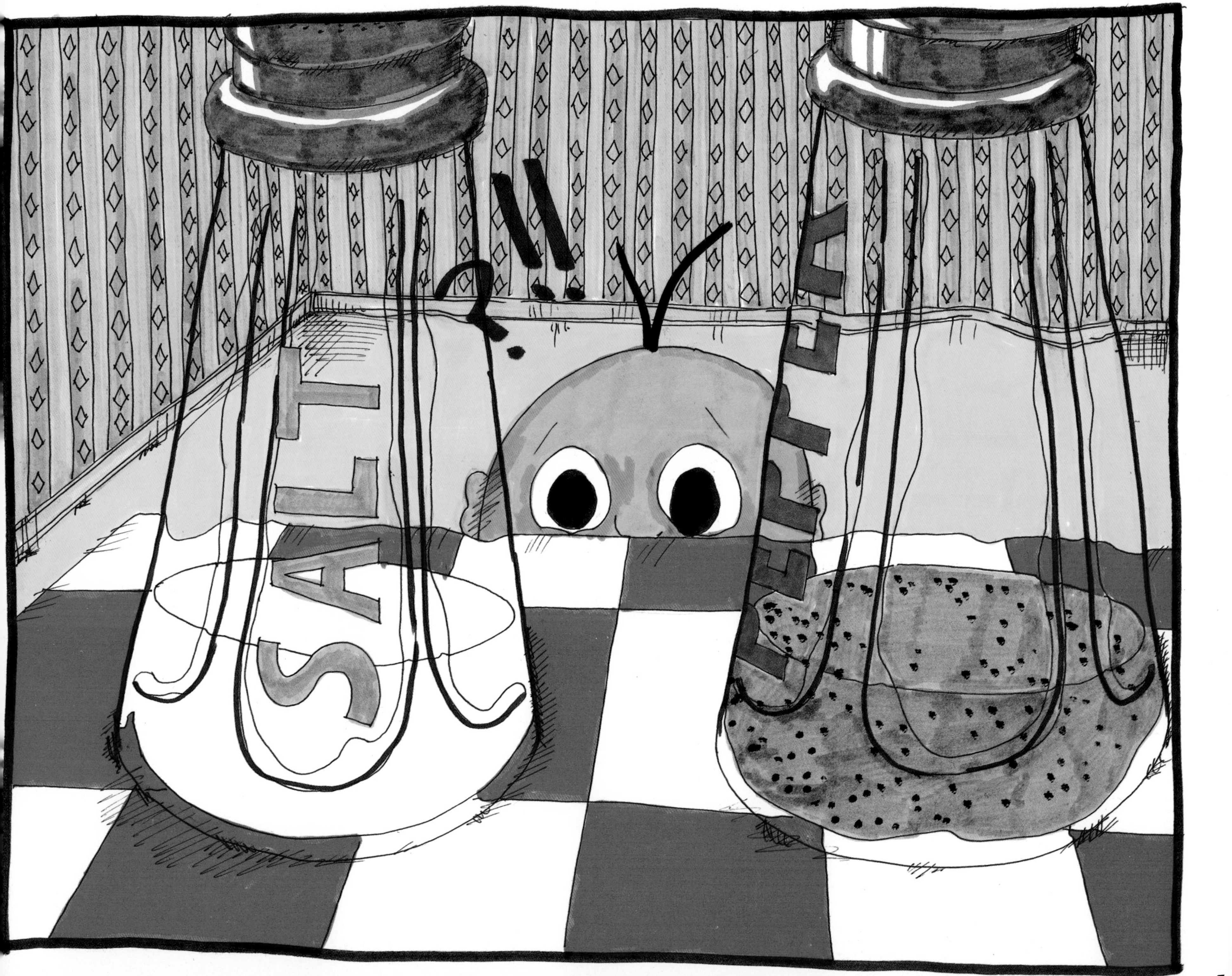
?!!
SALT
PEPPER

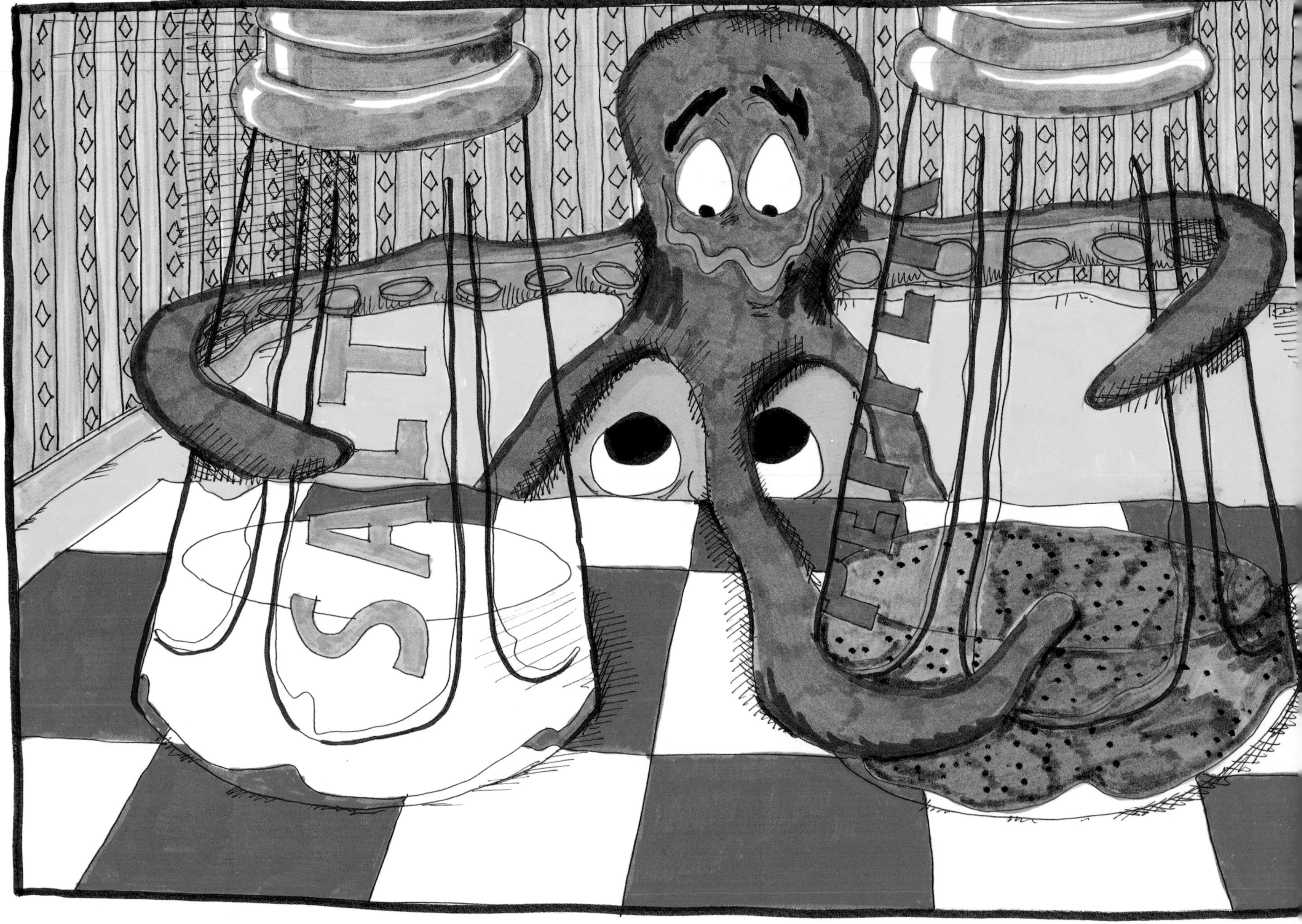
SALT

His Mom said, "Oh, Howard, you've got monsters on the brain!"

That was a pretty spooky thing for Howard to think about.

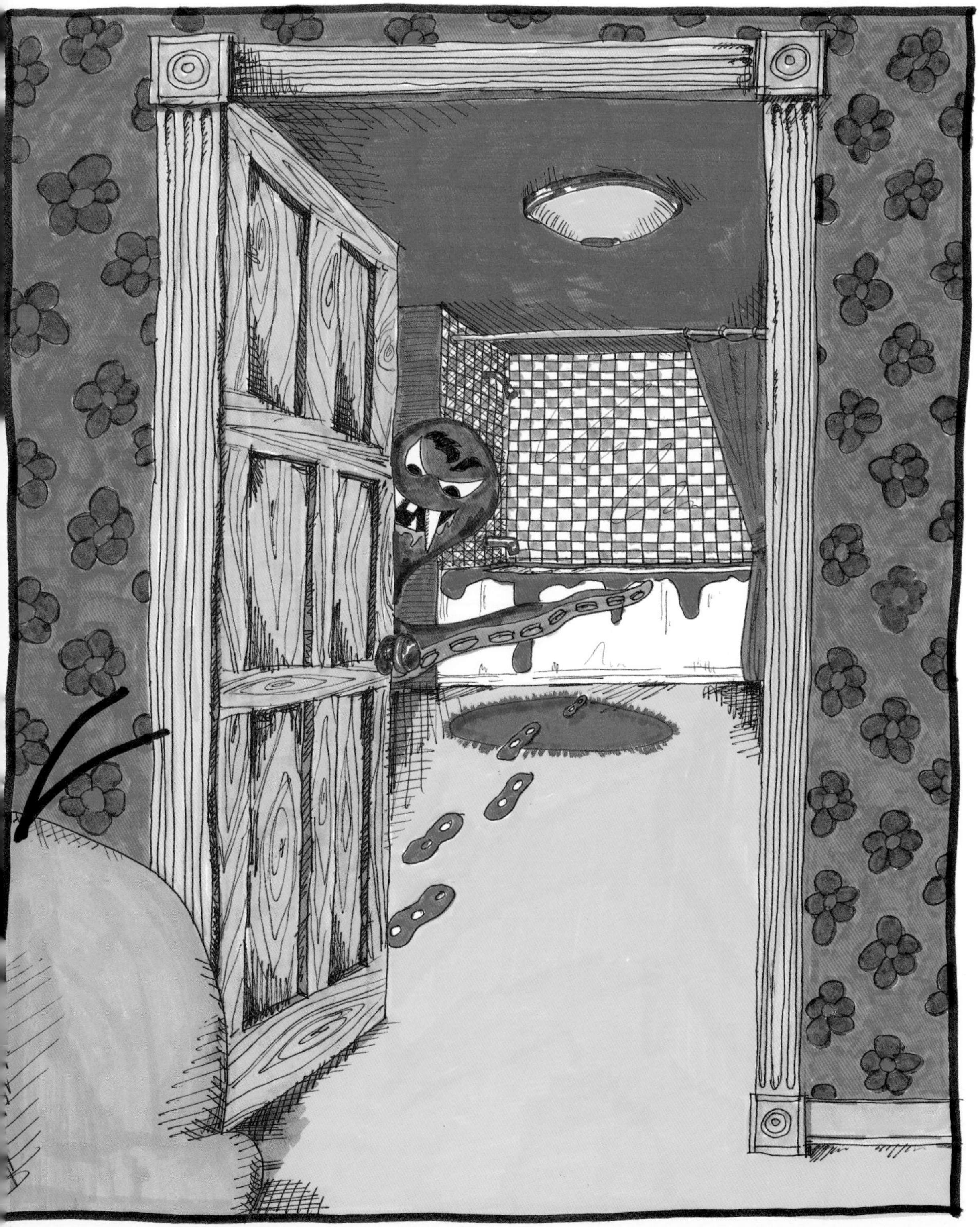

Howard was pretty sure that a monster might live in his bathtub.

Howard told his Mom, but she just said, "Howard Wise, you have a really wonderful imagination."

And Howard thought to himself, "Yes, I do, but I know that you think that I'm making all of this up."

Howard had to go to the bathroom, to use his potty chair (like a good boy, without any help), and, like always, he could SWEAR that he could feel that old monster watching him!

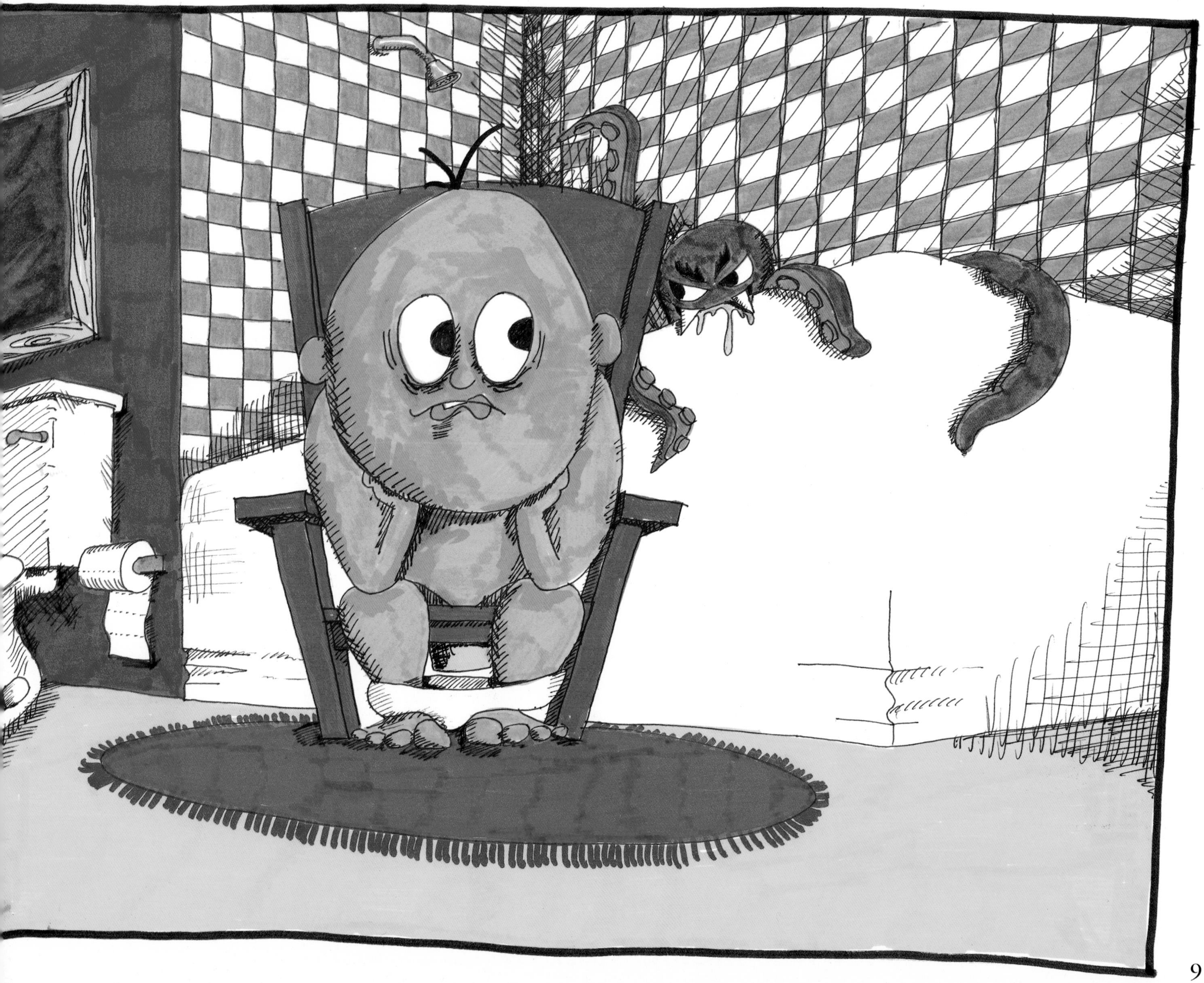

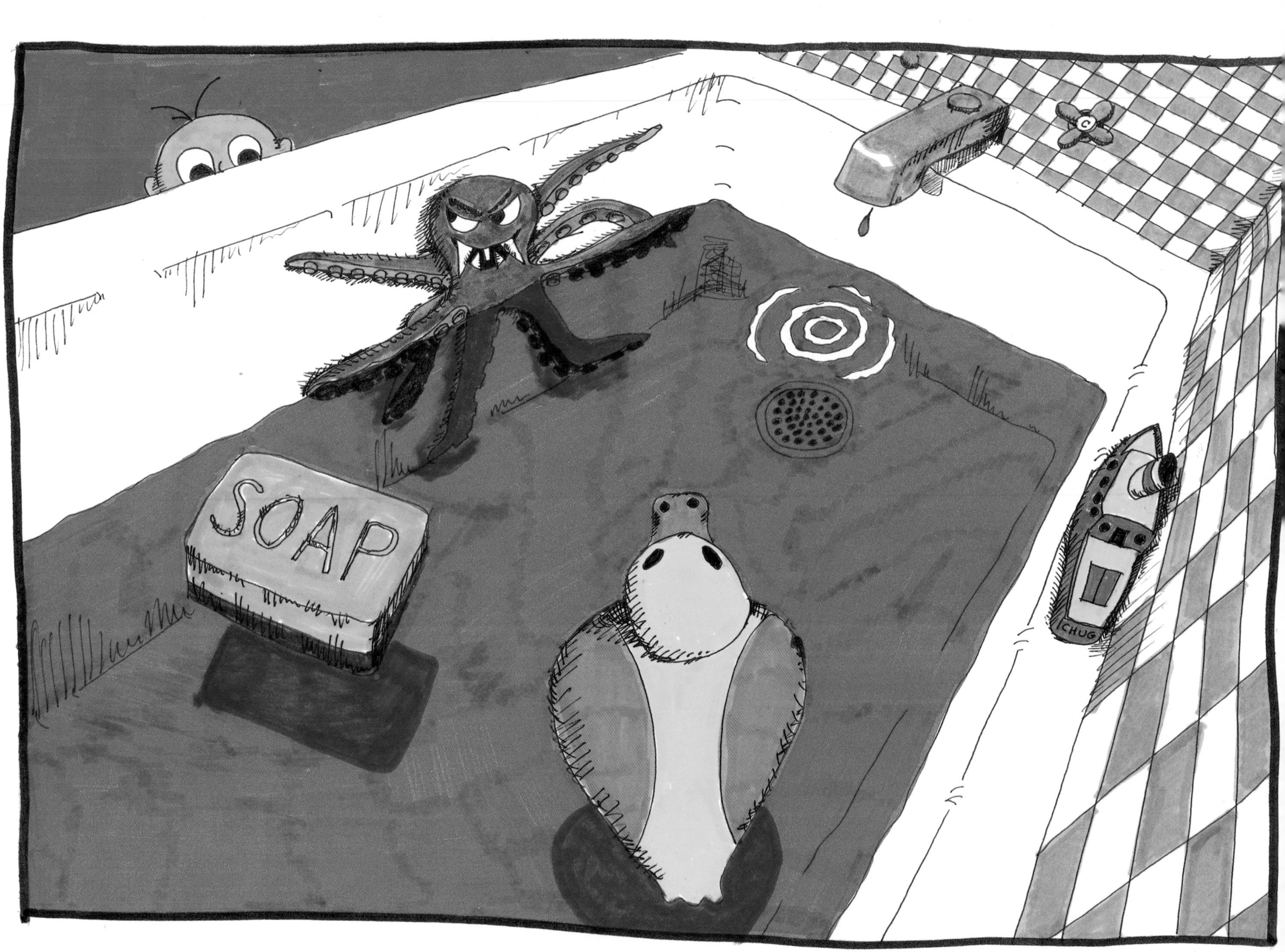

SOAP
CHUG

Howard jumped up, as soon as he could, to look, but that sneaky old monster was hiding, so Howard couldn't see it.

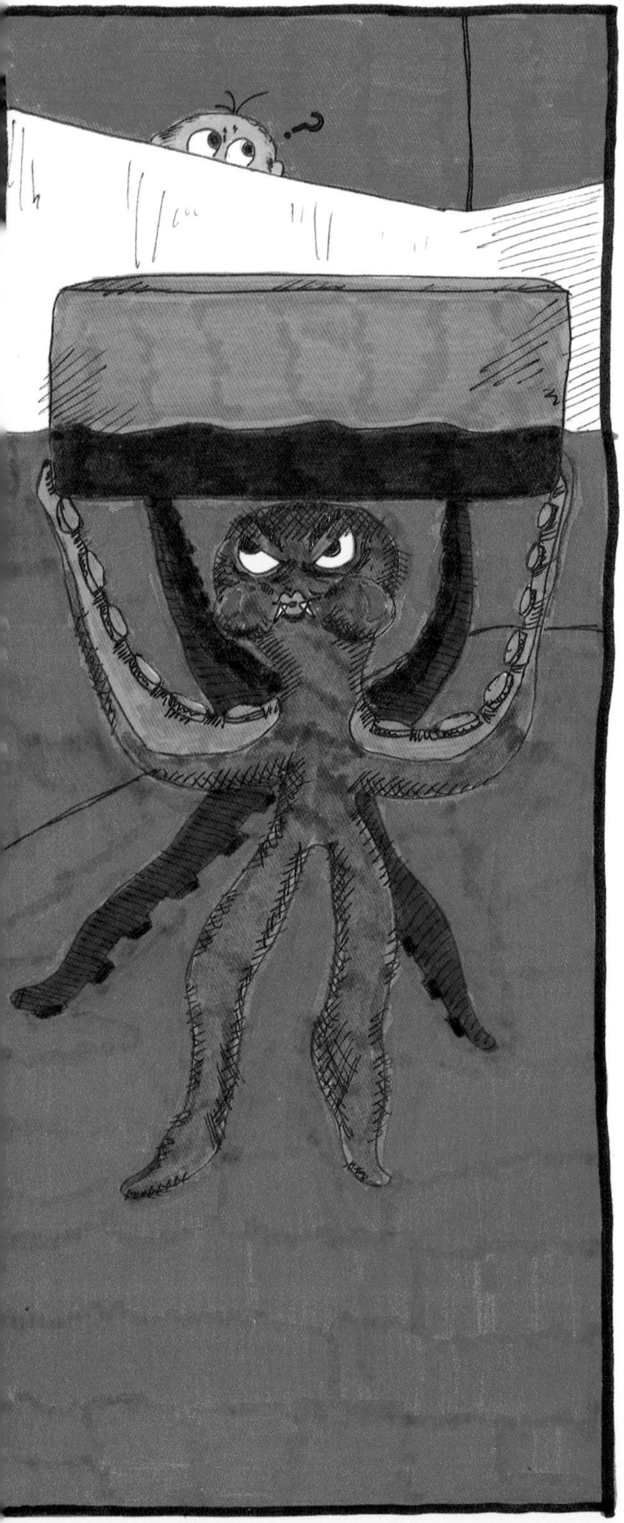

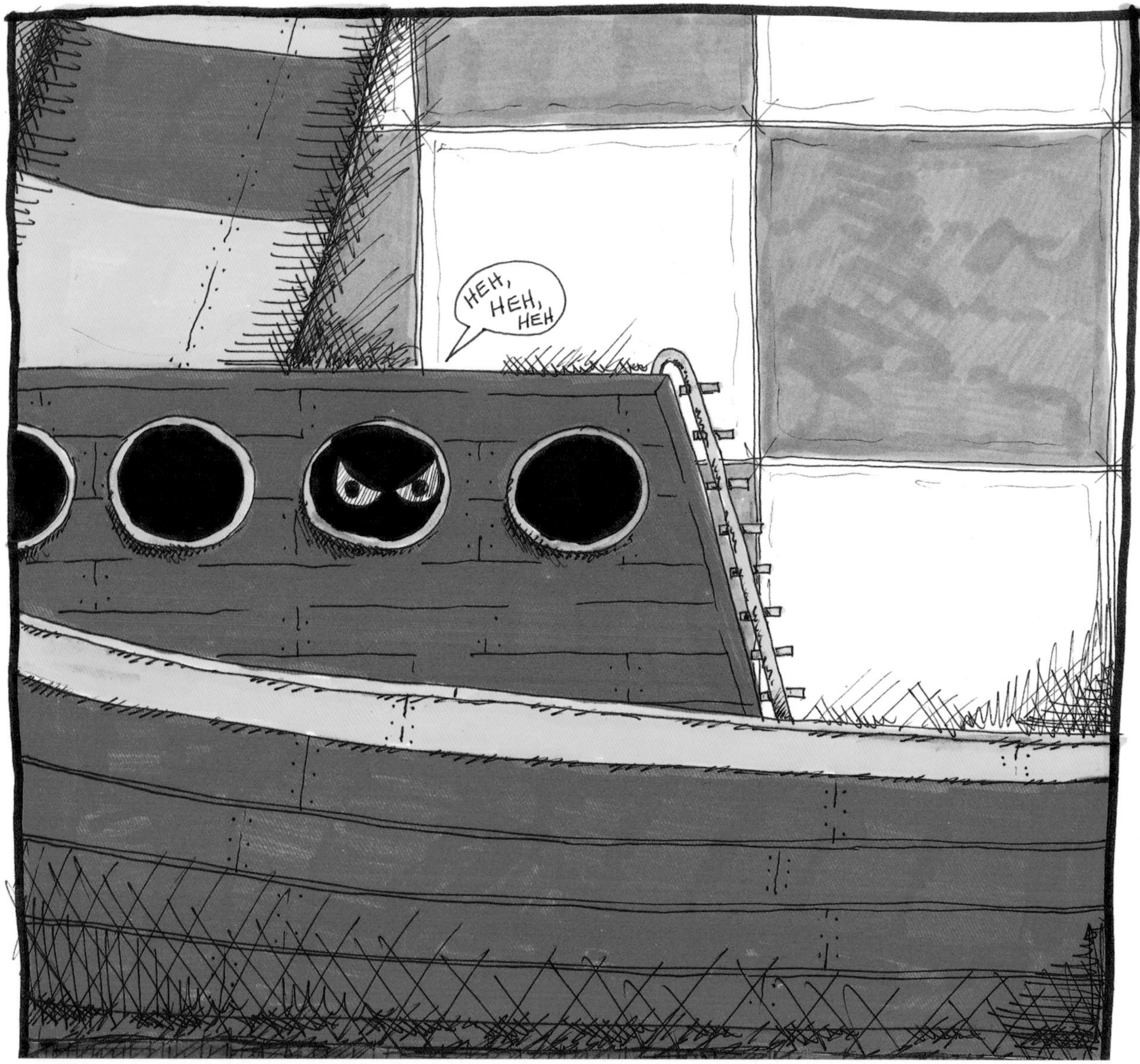
HEH,
HEH,
HEH

Maybe the monster was hiding under the big bar of soap floating in the tub.

Or, maybe the monster was hiding belowdeck on Howard's chuggy tug boat. What a sneak!

One thing was for sure! The poor Ducky was 'way too CHICKEN to tell Howard where that sneaky monster was hiding, because Ducky just knew that the monster would eat him... if he was a tattletale.

But...do you know what?

The Ducky was wrong!

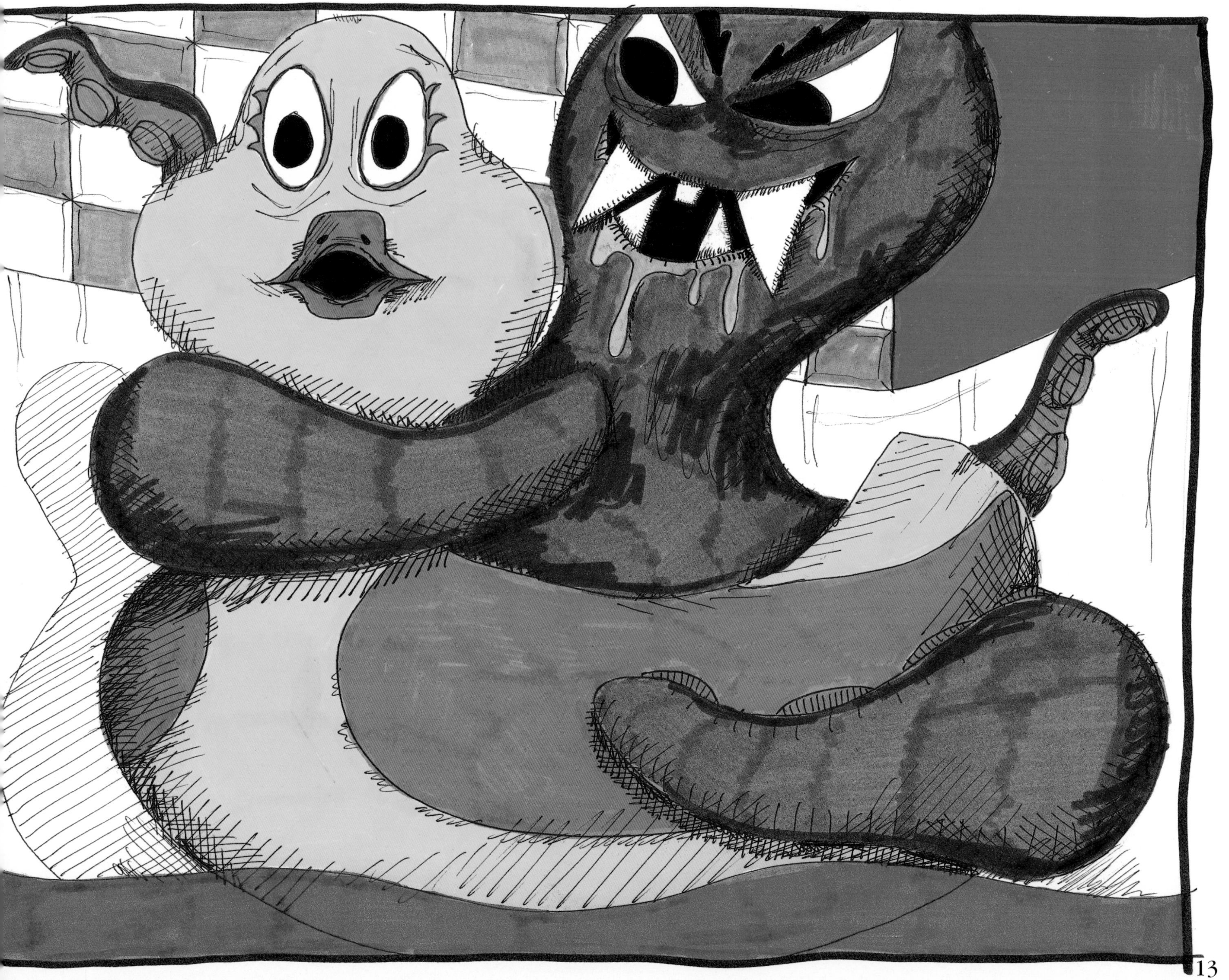

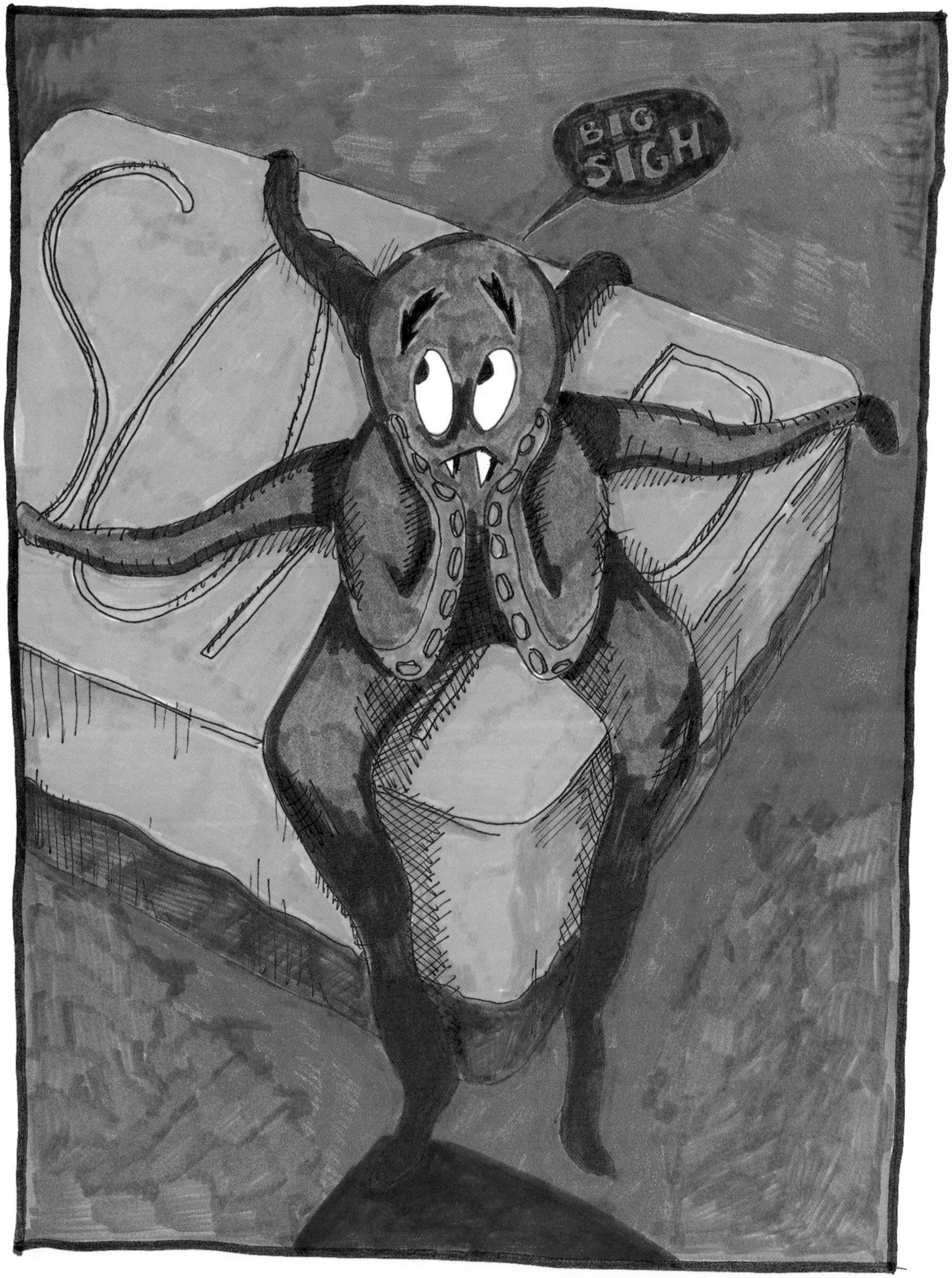
BIG SIGH

Because...the poor old sneaky monster was really just LONELY...and very very shy.

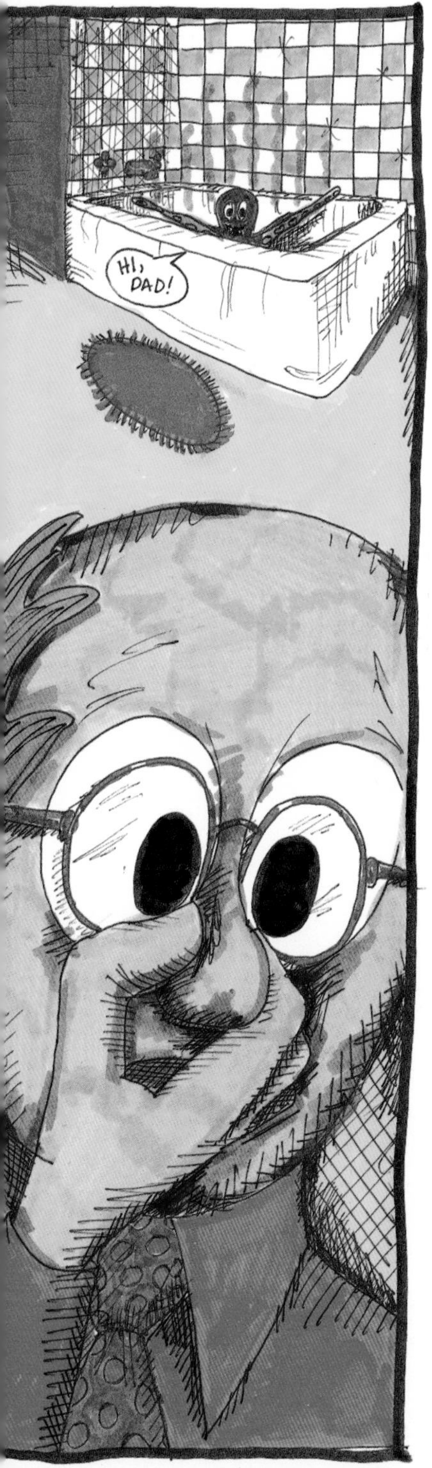
HI, DAD!

The monster hid from everybody, because it was afraid that the family might not like it. They might think that it was ugly and smelly. (Actually, it WAS pretty smelly, to human people. It smelled like a normal monster. That was o.k. when it was just hanging out with other monsters, but, it knew that Howard's Dad got pretty weird about smelly stuff in the house.)

So, it figured that Howard's parents might make the smelly little monster leave the warm, cuddly house, and go to live outside.

Where the (gulp) CATS were!

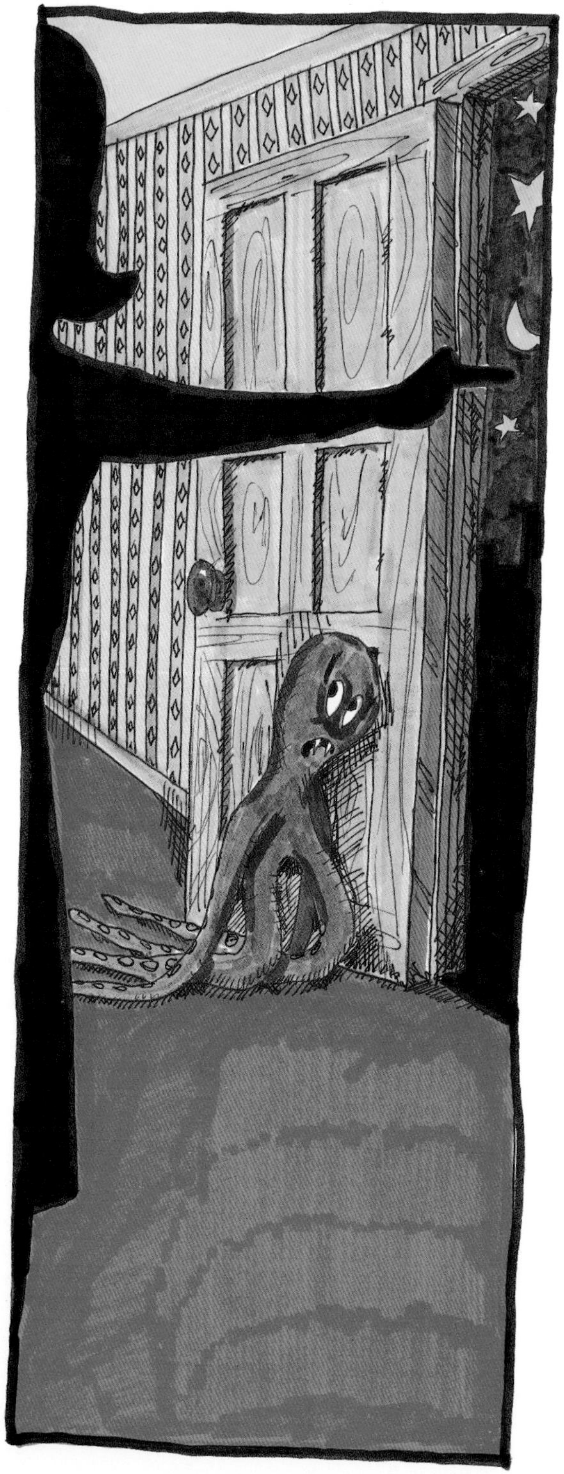

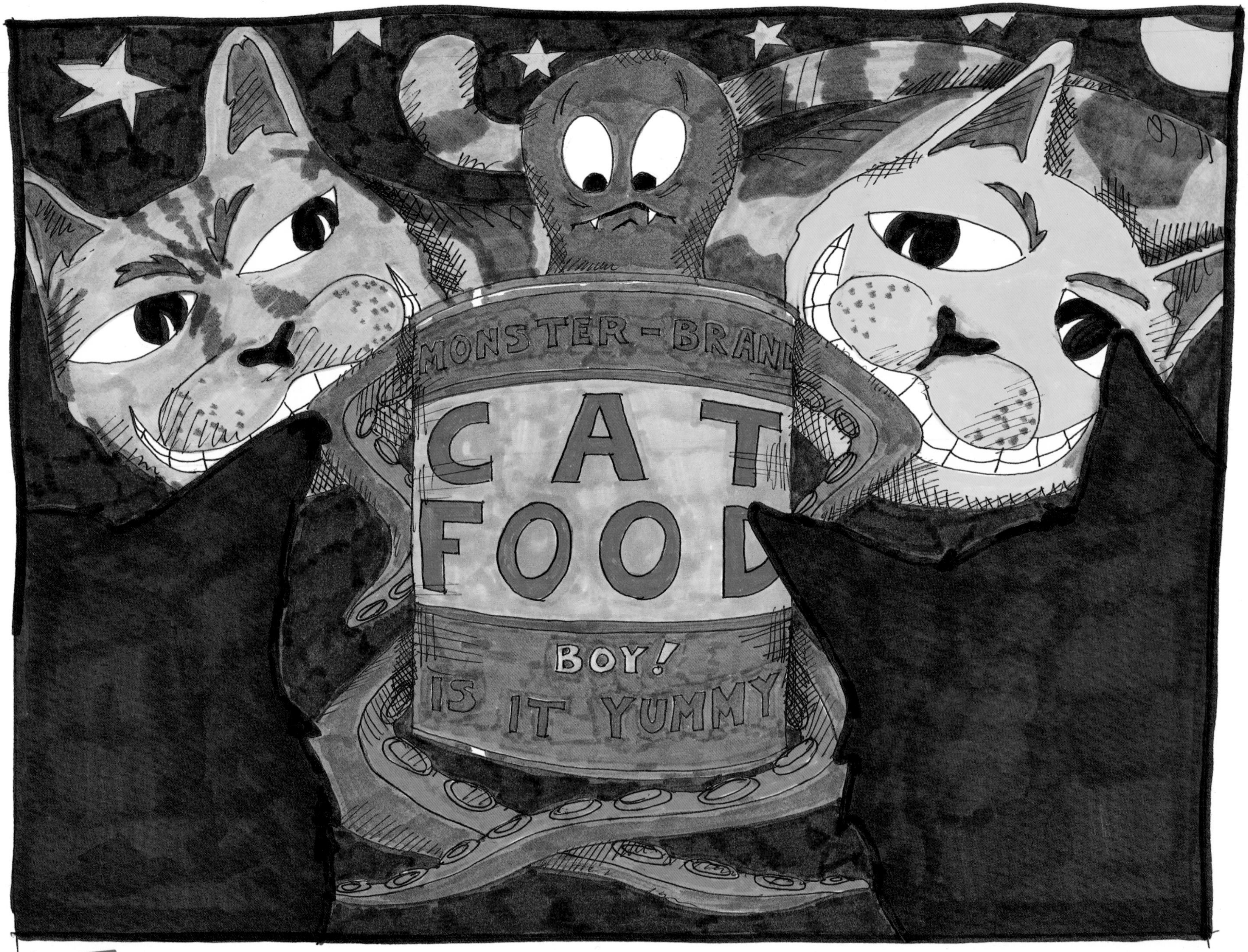
MONSTER-BRAND
CAT
FOOD
BOY!
IS IT YUMMY

Those mean old creepy-cats didn't think that it smelled stinky.

 Those creepy-cats thought that the little monster smelled like FOOD!

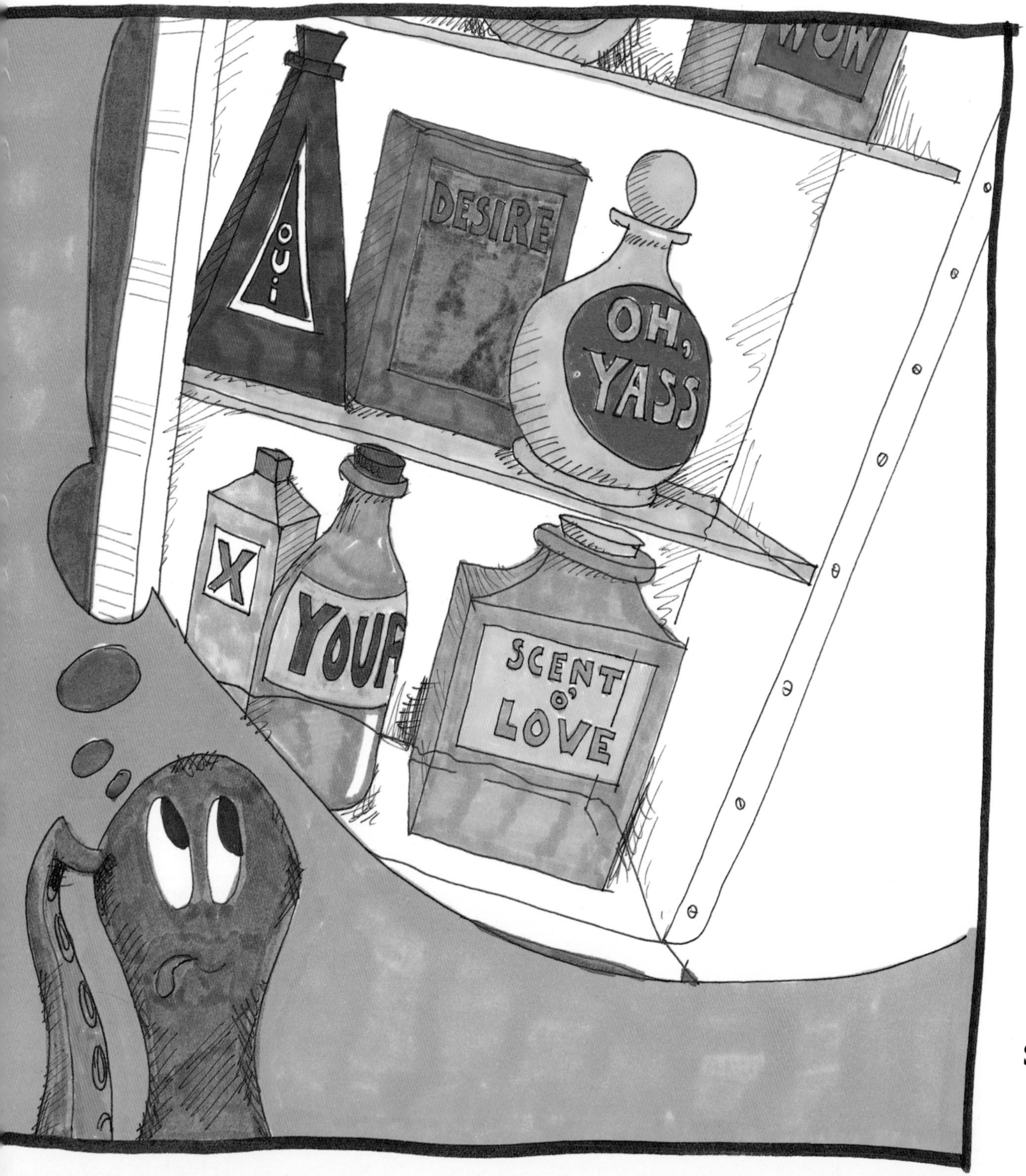
WOW
DESIRE
OUI
OH, YASS
X
YOUR
SCENT O' LOVE

So, the monster thought and thought.

"Hmmm…if I didn't smell so bad, maybe Mom and Dad would let me live in the bathtub."

That was when it remembered… the medicine chest! Mom had lots of sweet smelling perfumes in there. Dad always liked Mom a lot, when she sprayed on some of that stuff.

Maybe the same sweet smelly perfume would work on the monster?

So...the sneaky-smelly monster crept down the hallway, and into Mom and Dad's bathroom.

Standing up tall on it's tippy-toe tentacles, it reached out a long purple arm towards the medicine chest.

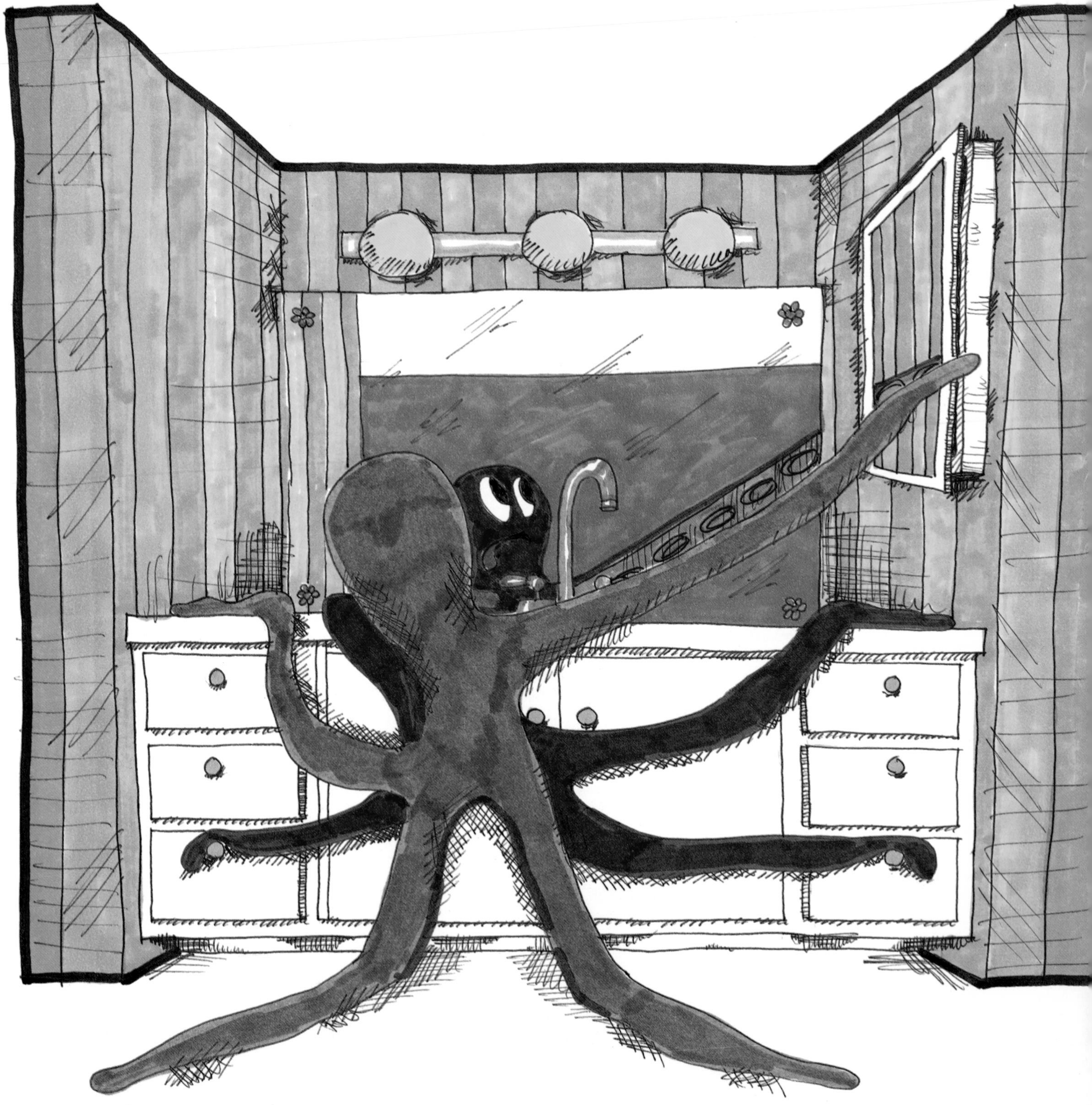

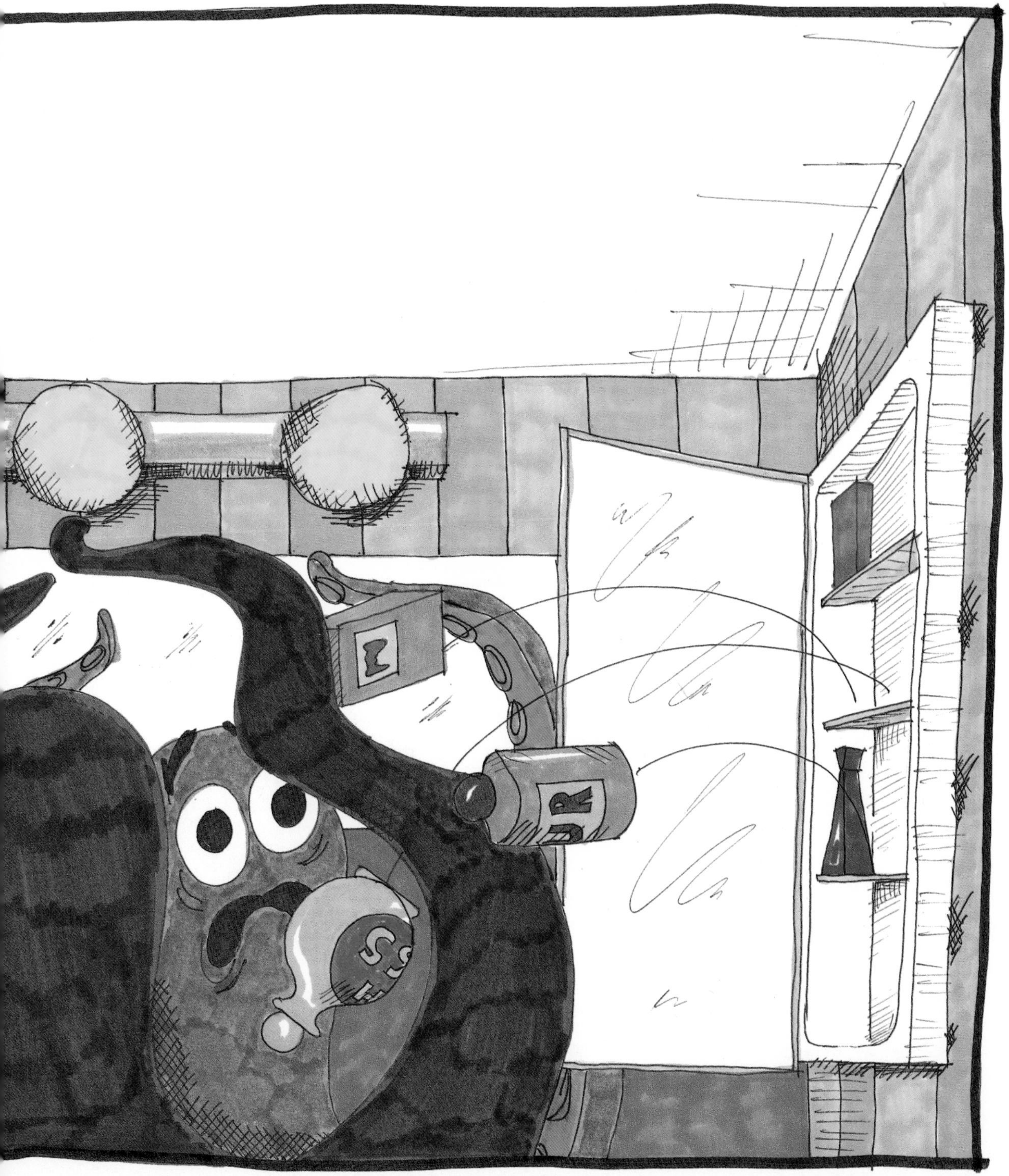

But...

The silly old stinkpot monster was in 'way, 'way too much of a hurry. It knocked over some of the bottles, and...Crash! Bam! Boom!..all of the jars and bottles came jumping and bumping their way out of the cabinet!

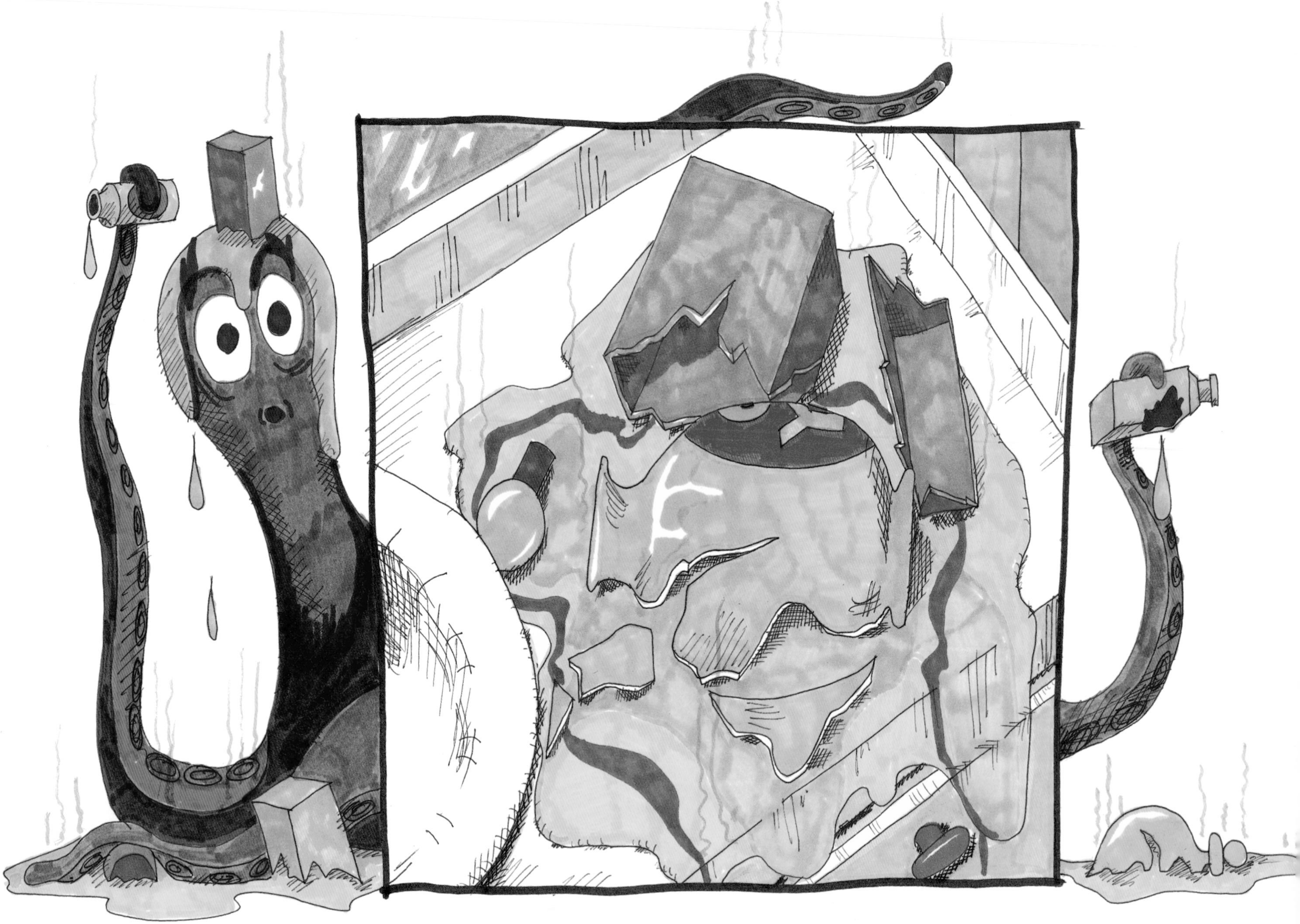

JUMPING CAT WHISKERS! Now Howard's parents were going to be REALLY angry

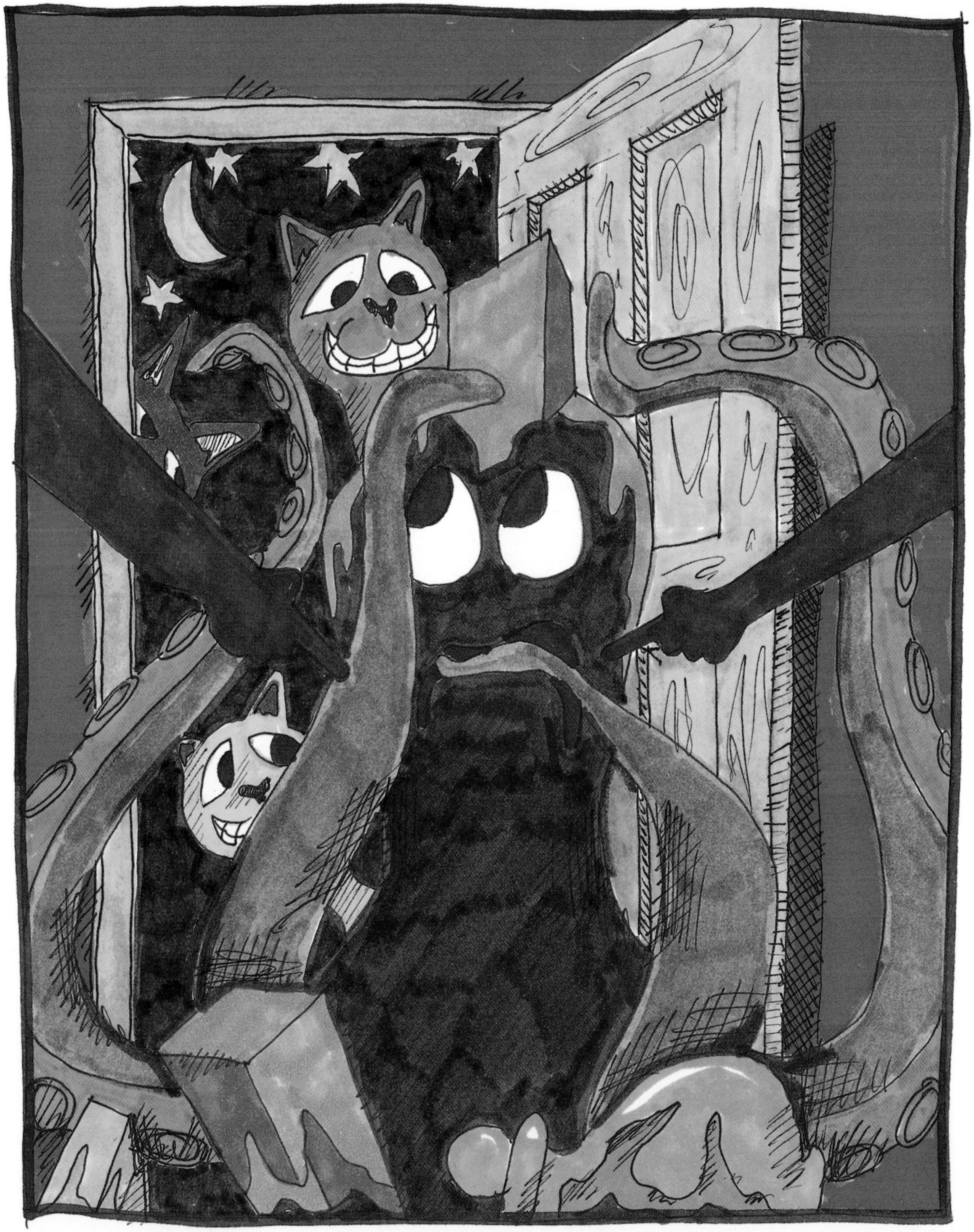

CREEPY CAT COUNTRY, FOR SURE!

"Wait a monster-minute!", it thought. "I can blame this on Howard! Yeah!"

With the one unbroken bottle of perfume, that old stinky-socks monster slithered into Howard's room, while he was asleep. Creeping over on it's tippy-toe tentacles, it reached in and sprayed and sprayed and SPRAYED the sweet-smelling perfume, all over Howard. Now, Howard's parents would know for sure that SOMEHOW, Howard Wise had made the big mess!

"Heh, heh, heh.", thought the monster.

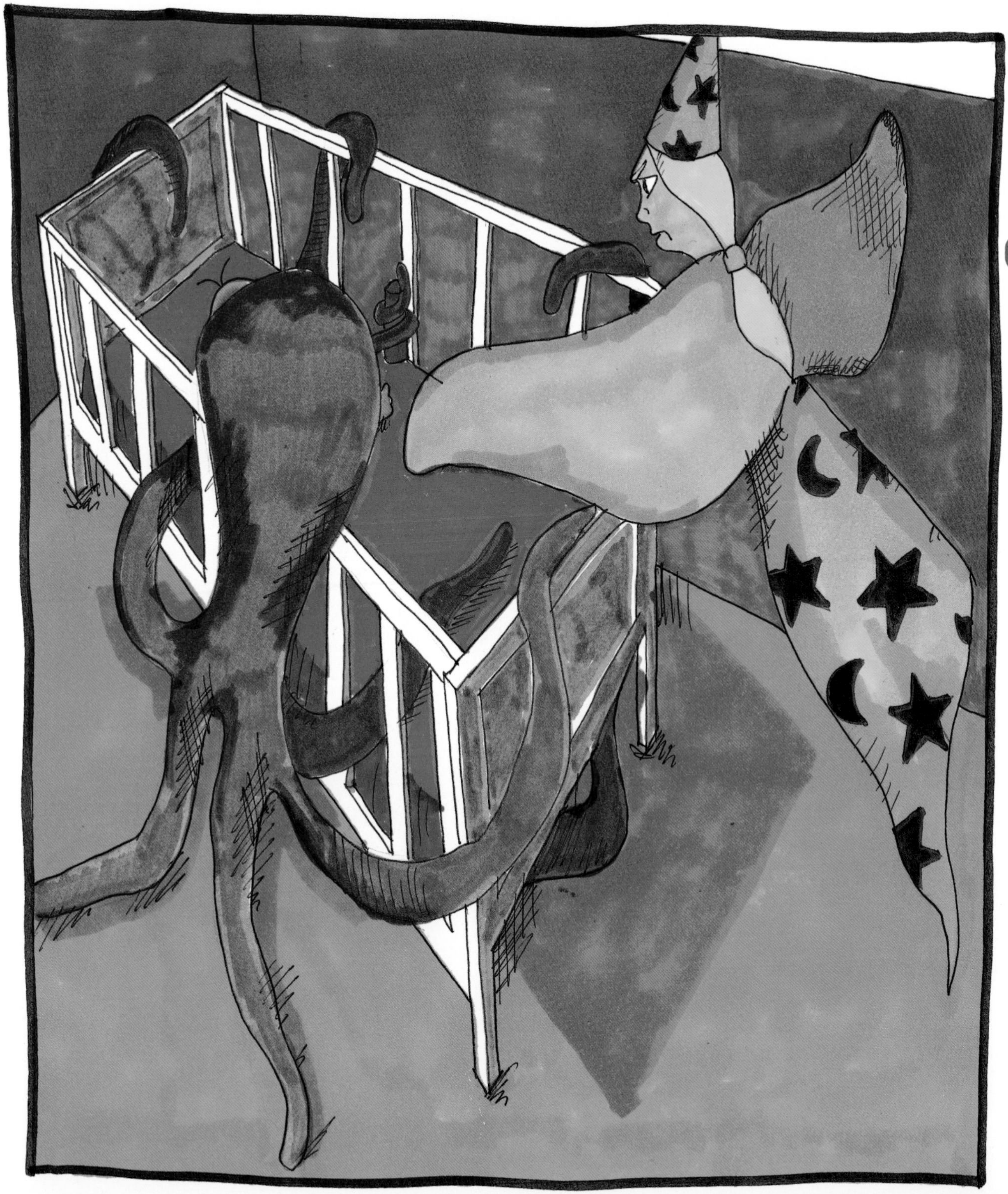

" Not so fast, Mr. Cat-Bait!"

Garnet, the Gracious Good Fairy, who watches over all good boys and girls when they are asleep, was flying over, on patrol, when she saw what happened.

"You've got to learn how to clean up your OWN messes, Mr. Smelly-Belly!", she shouted. "Take this!"

Suddenly, the surprised monster felt the room start to shudder and shak A fierce wind whipped around it's tippy-toe tentacles. Overhead, Garne was spinning around and around, gathering up magic lightning from the skies. Faster and faster, whirling FASTER and FASTER, shouting the magic incantation, "CROAKING FROGS AND SLIMY SNAKES ... SNEAKY MONSTERS, I CANNOT TAKE!"

Garnet SNAPPED her golden pony-tail, and, with a bold crash of lightnin BOOM!, she changed that sneak-pot monster into A BIG PURPLE MOP!

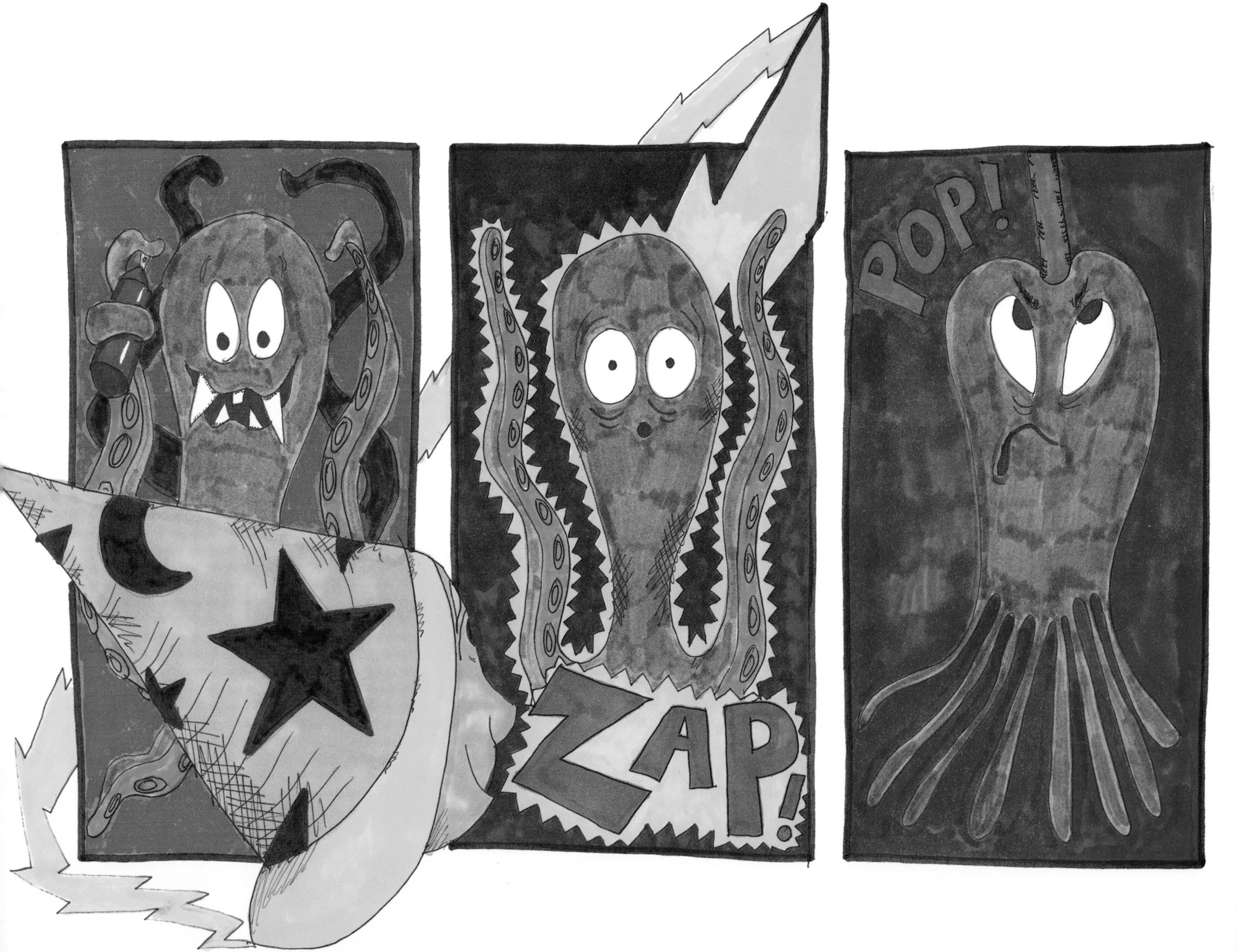
ZAP!
POP!

And THEN, flying down low over Howard, who had slept right through all
of the magic and commotion, Garnet flapped her tiny wings together,
furiously, and quickly blew all of the smelly perfume off of Howard Wise,
before he woke up.

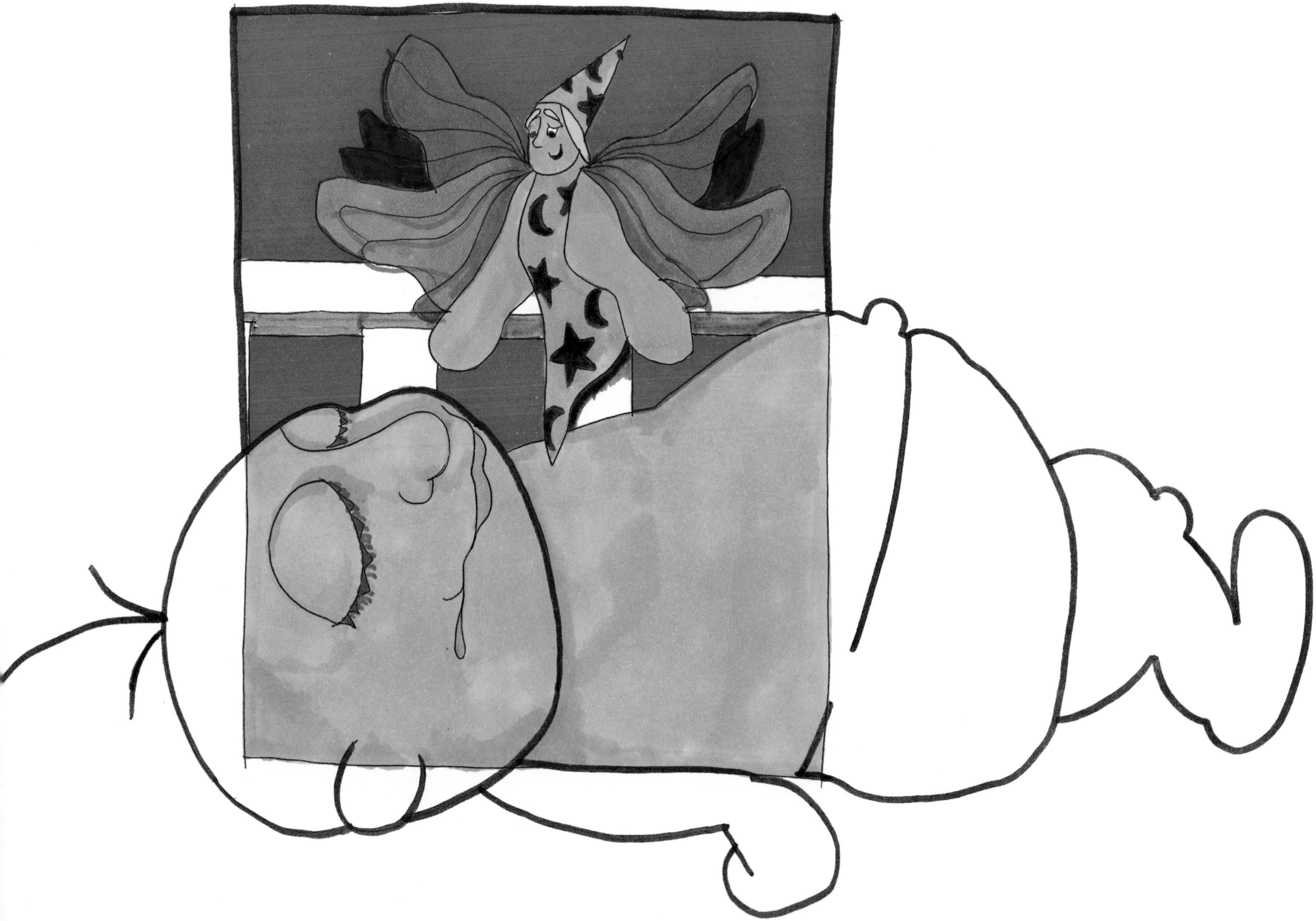

"Who in the world could have done this?!?", cried Mom. "And what made those funny looking tracks on the floor? I'm going to follow those tracks, and make somebody clean up this mess!"

Mom was very, very angry as she followed the trail of monster tracks down the hall, into Howard's room, and, across the room, into Howard's closet.

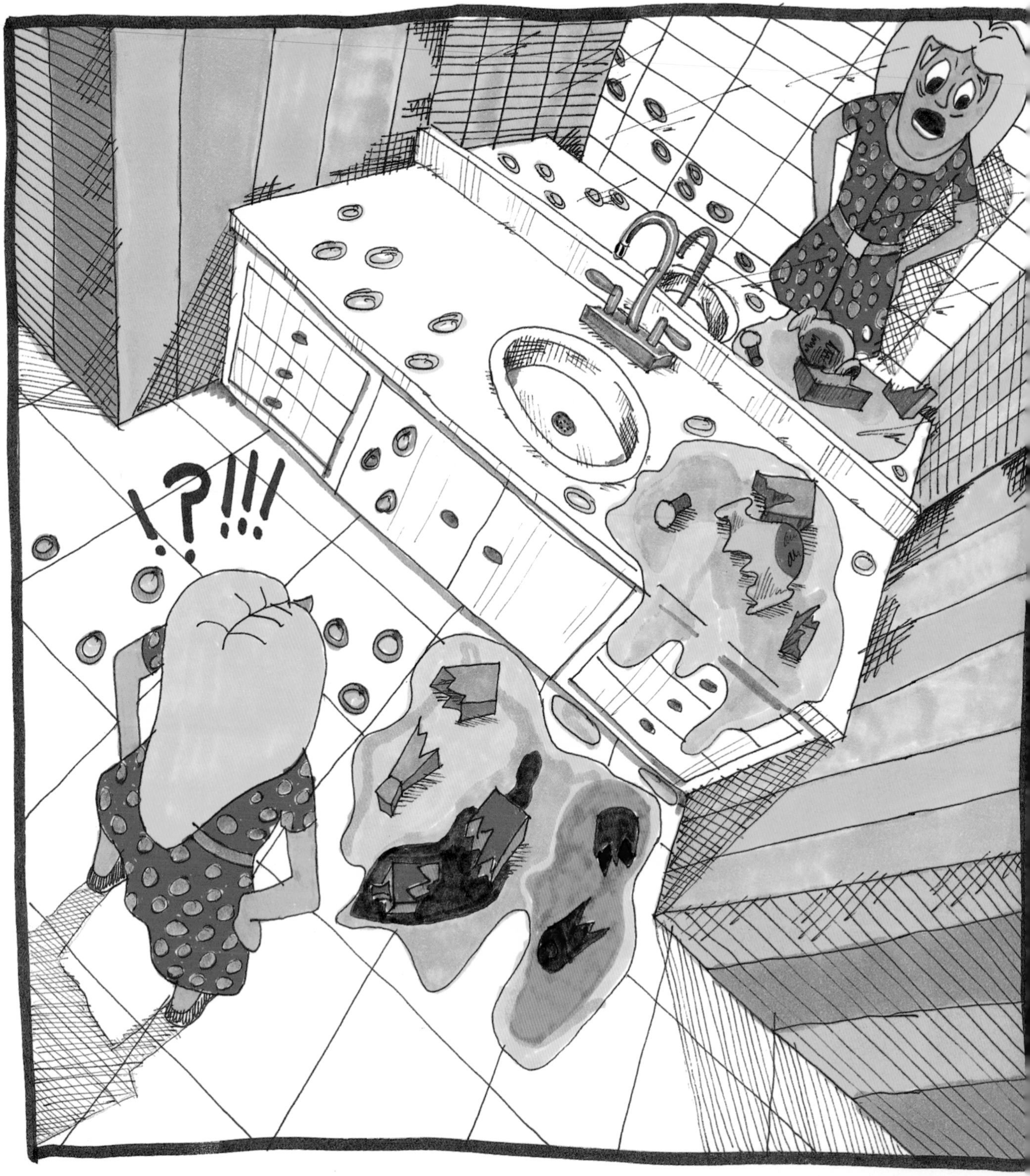
!?!!!

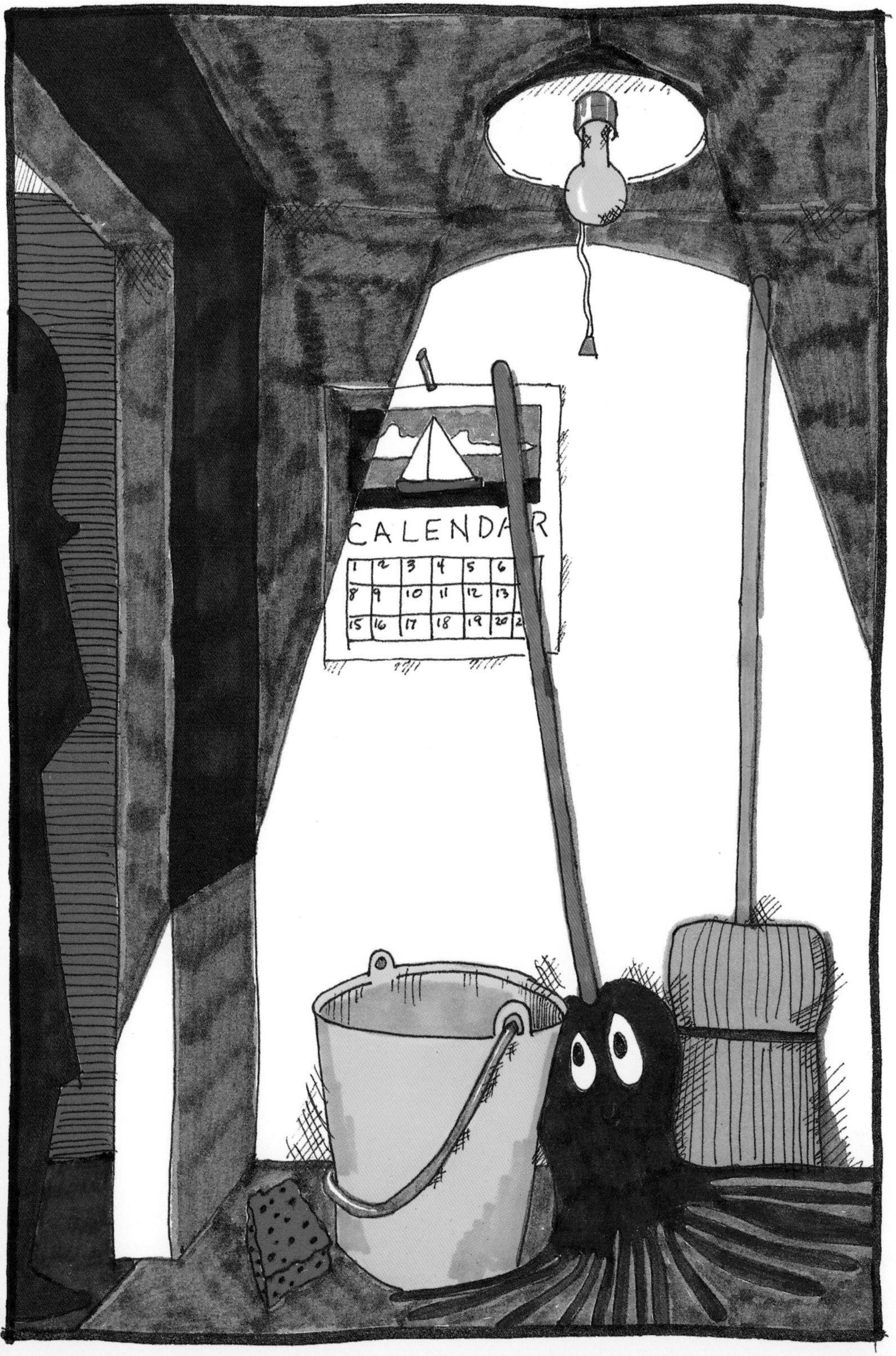
CALENDAR

"I'm going to find out just WHO made that mess, and these funny-looking tracks!", Mom fumed, as she JERKED open the door to the closet.

But, to her surprise, there was nothing in the closet but a broom and a sponge, and a shiny yellow bucket...and, a BIG PURPLE MOP.

"Hmmm...", Mom thought. "That big purple mop would be just PERFECT to help me clean up that huge mess."

And, that's how it ended.

Howard's sneaky-stinky old monster was gone, and it never bothered Howard to go to the bathroom alone, ever again.

The monster, (who was now a big purple mop) didn't smell stinky anymore, after helping Mom to clean up all of the sweet-smelling pefume mess.

Also, it didn't have to worry about having to live outside, in creepy-cat country, ever, ever again.

So...everybody ended up very, very, VERY happy, after all.

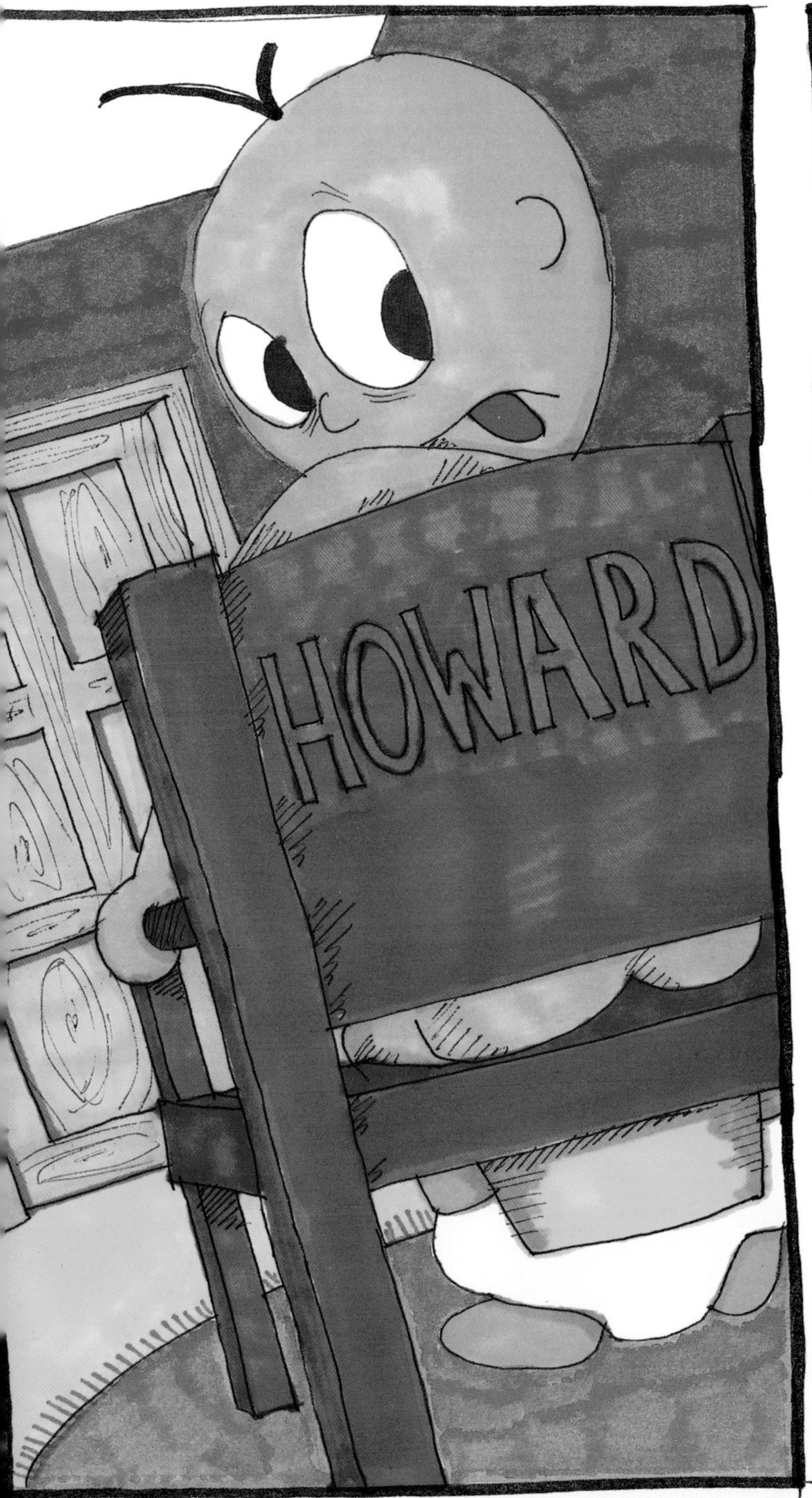
HOWARD

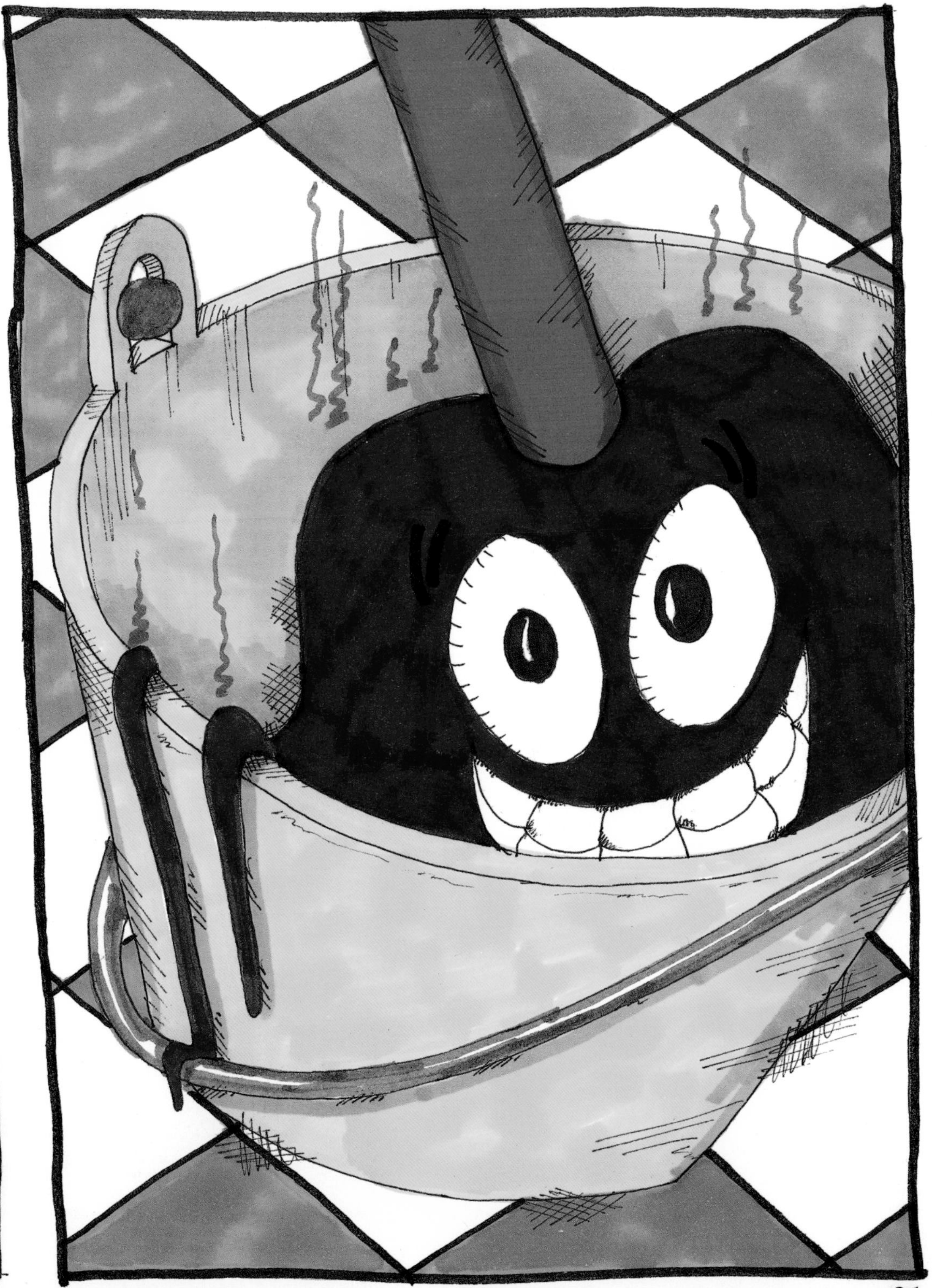

Well...
ALMOST everybody.

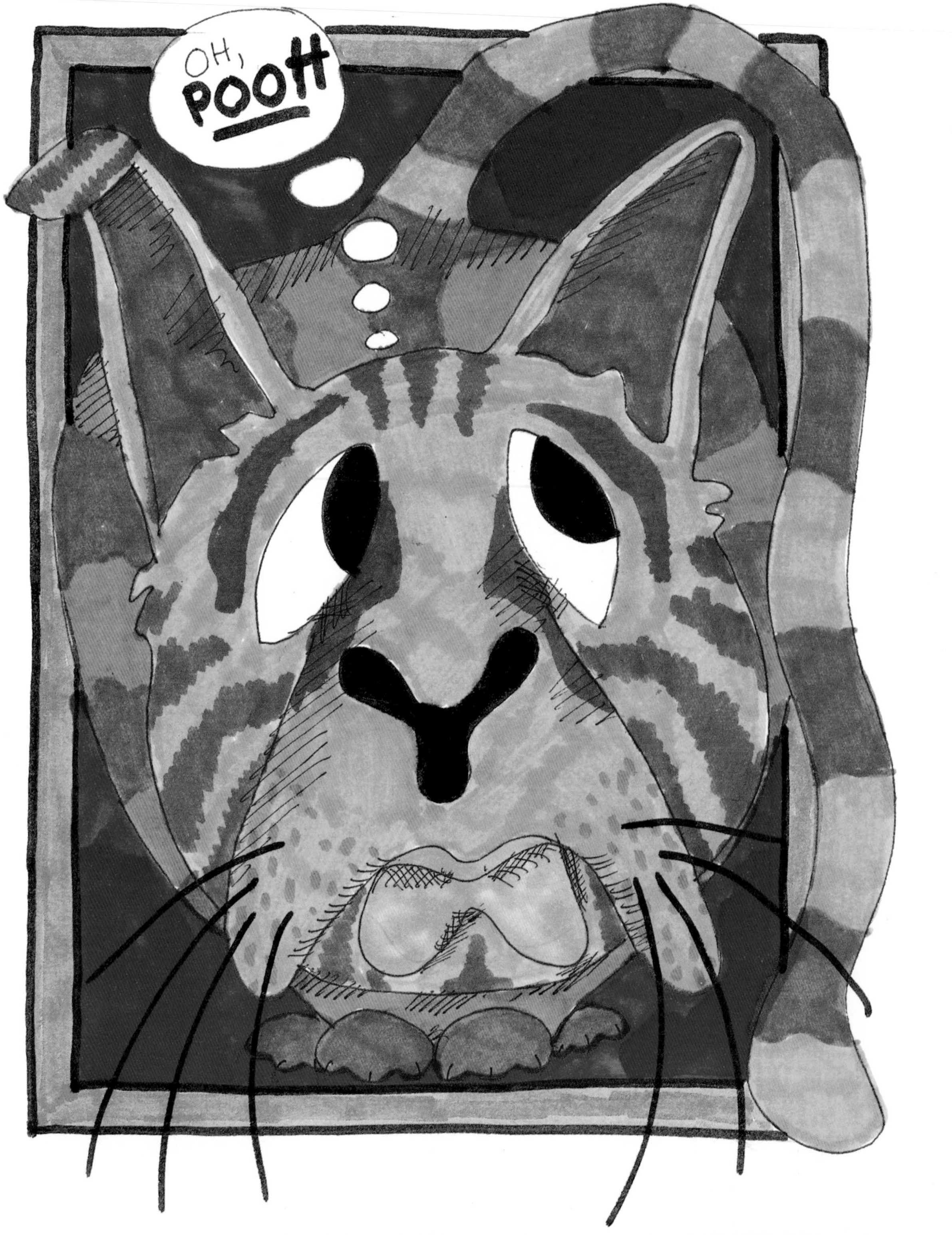
OH, POOH

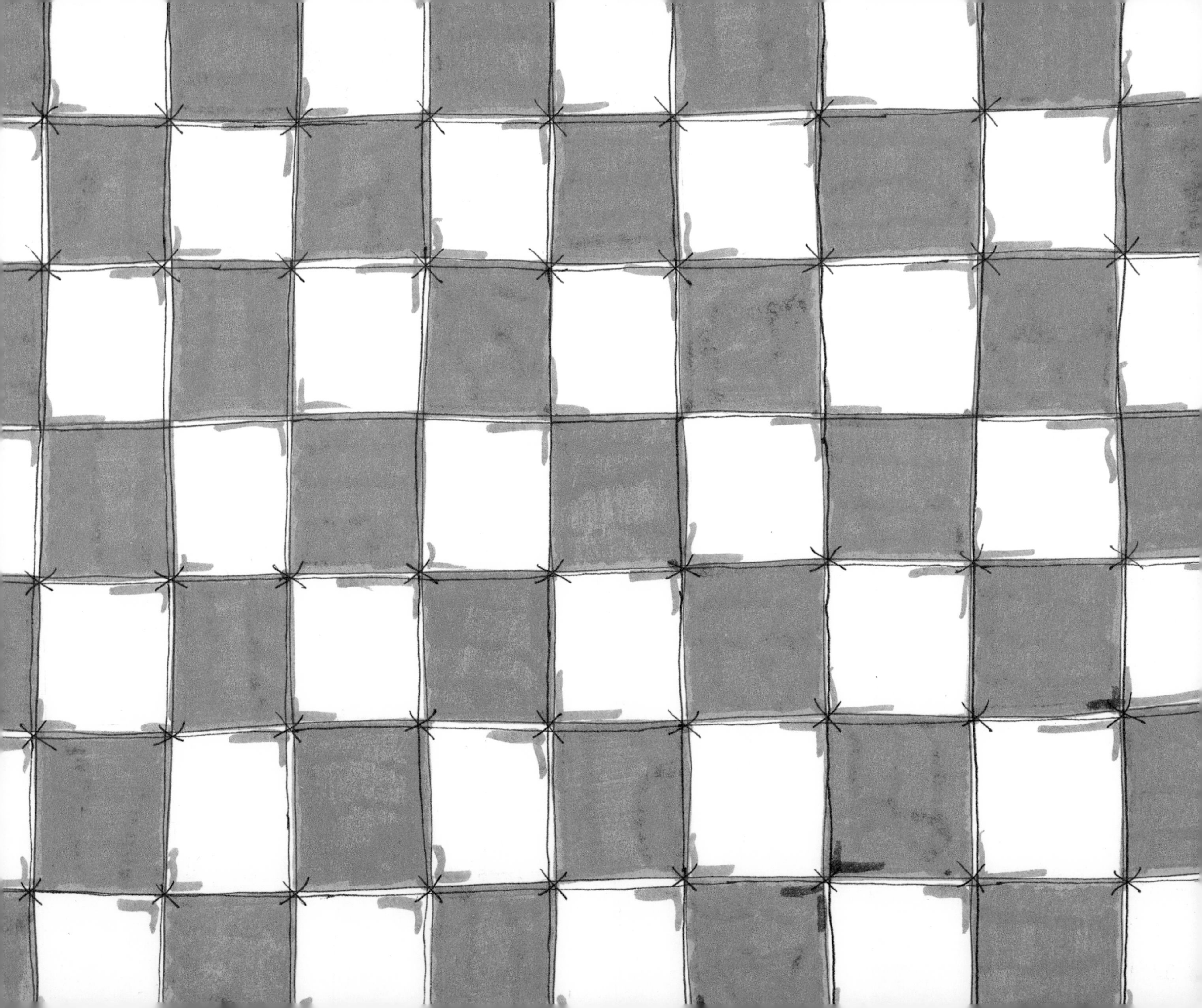

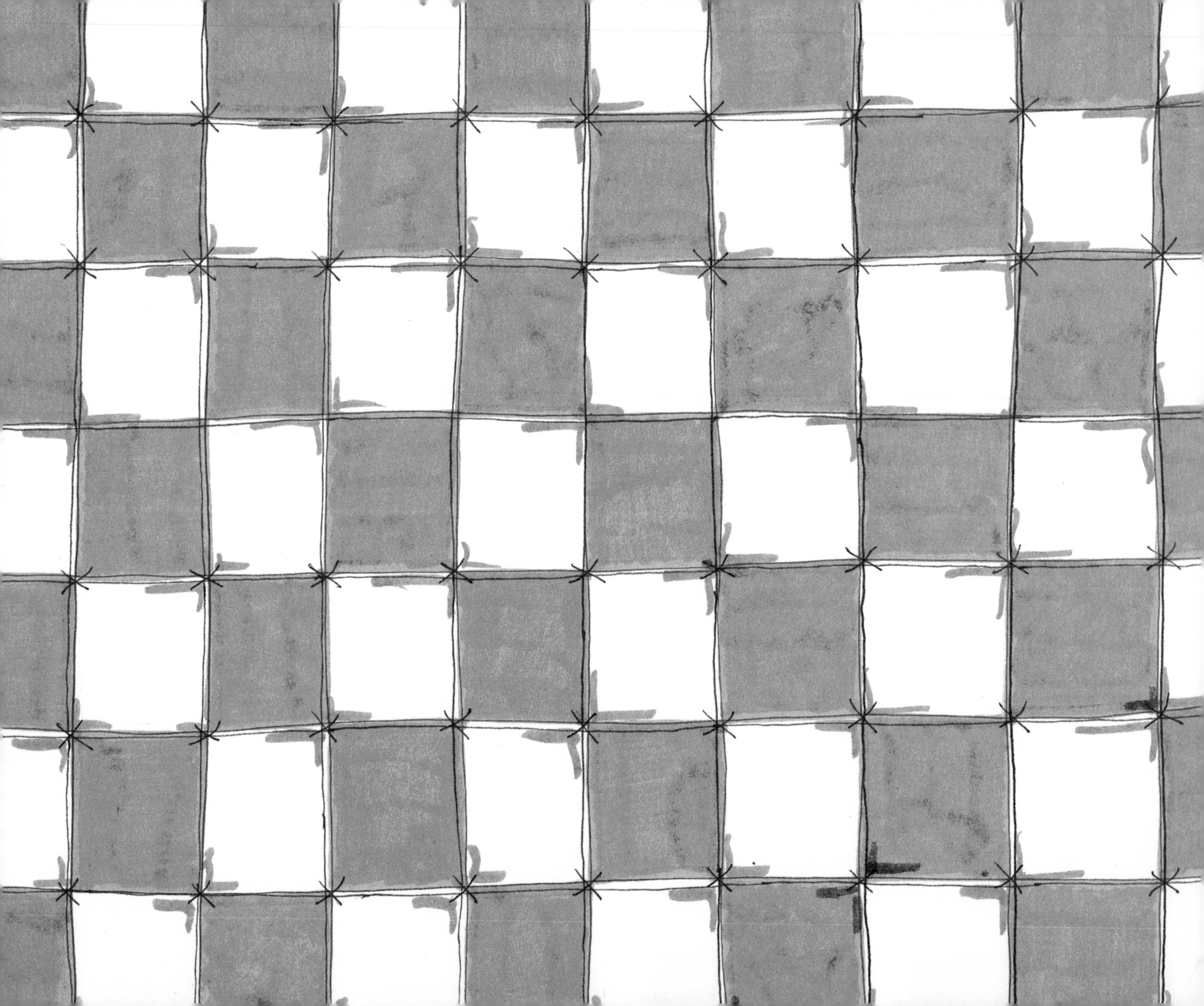